FLAMES THAT MELT

Tish Carlisle returns from Tennessee to clear out her late father's house in Cornwall — to several surprises. The first is the woman and baby she discovers living there and the second is her father's solicitor, Nico De Burgh, who was Tish's first love. Nico fights their renewed attraction because of a promise made to his foster father but Tish won't give up on him. They must share their secrets before they have any chance of a loving future together . . .

Books by Angela Britnell
in the Linford Romance Library:

HUSHED WORDS

ANGELA BRITNELL

◆

FLAMES THAT MELT

Complete and Unabridged

LINFORD
Leicester

First published in Great Britain

First Linford Edition
published 2013

Copyright © 2012 by Angela Britnell

A catalogue record for this book is available
from the British Library.

ISBN 978–1–4448–1791–1

Published by
F. A. Thorpe (Publishing)
Anstey, Leicestershire

Set by Words & Graphics Ltd.
Anstey, Leicestershire
Printed and bound in Great Britain by
T. J. International Ltd., Padstow, Cornwall

This book is printed on acid-free paper

SPECIAL MESSAGE TO READERS

THE ULVERSCROFT FOUNDATION
(registered UK charity number 264873)

was established in 1972 to provide funds for research, diagnosis and treatment of eye diseases. Examples of major projects funded by the Ulverscroft Foundation are:-

- The Children's Eye Unit at Moorfields Eye Hospital, London
- The Ulverscroft Children's Eye Unit at Great Ormond Street Hospital for Sick Children
- Funding research into eye diseases and treatment at the Department of Ophthalmology, University of Leicester
- The Ulverscroft Vision Research Group, Institute of Child Health
- Twin operating theatres at the Western Ophthalmic Hospital, London
- The Chair of Ophthalmology at the Royal Australian College of Ophthalmologists

You can help further the work of the Foundation by making a donation or leaving a legacy. Every contribution is gratefully received. If you would like to help support the Foundation or require further information, please contact:

THE ULVERSCROFT FOUNDATION
The Green, Bradgate Road, Anstey
Leicester LE7 7FU, England
Tel: (0116) 236 4325

website: www.foundation.ulverscroft.com

1

The car stalled again and Tish let out a very unladylike curse, thankful that her mother couldn't hear from four thousand miles away. Manual transmission cars, death-defying roundabouts and pathetic road signs — three good reasons she was determined never to drive outside the States again. Next time she'd use public transportation.

Next time? She must be out of her freakin' mind. As soon as she'd sorted things out here, it'd be the first plane back to Nashville for her.

She restarted the stupid car and with a grinding jerk managed to get going. Stubbornly she'd ignored her mother's advice to leave it up to the lawyer to clear the house and now number six, Beach Road was around the next corner.

Tish allowed the car to sputter and

die outside the front door. She flipped down the mirror on the visor and cringed. Definitely not her usual fashionable self . . . but an empty house wasn't going to care. Opening the car door, she grabbed her tote bag and keys and stepped out. Staring up at the house she'd left fourteen years before, the impulse to turn around and drive back to London was almost overwhelming.

Sucking in a deep breath of fresh, salty air for courage, Tish resolved not to be a wimp and strode up the gravel path, surprised to note the fresh white paint, glossy black front door and neat, well-kept garden. She stuck her key in the latch and was startled when the door instantly flew open.

'I should've known you wouldn't waste any time coming now he's dead. You didn't bother when he was alive, did you?'

A red-faced blonde woman glared out at her and Tish took a step backwards.

2

'Don't you have a tongue in your head? If you think you're throwing us out with no warning you've another thought coming.'

Tish struggled to collect her senses while she sized up the woman — maybe about forty, with bleached hair, a good figure and a pretty enough face had it not been screwed up with fury.

'I'm sorry. I assumed the house was empty. Who are you?'

Are squatters usually this aggressive? she wondered.

'I'm Annie Treloare. Who the hell did you think I was? The housekeeper? I told Frank to sort this out, but he always put it off. Typical bloody man.'

Annie Treloare? What the hell?

'Could I come in?' Tish asked cautiously.

'You own the house now, so I can hardly stop you. You'd better be quiet because if you wake the baby I'll string you up — he didn't give me a minute's sleep last night.'

Tish stared, caught off guard. 'Baby?'

3

Annie rolled her eyes. 'Oh, wonderful. Didn't your father tell you *anything*?'

Obviously not. Tish shrugged and stepped into the cool, dim hallway. She should have listened to her mother.

★   ★   ★

'I'm expecting a Miss Treloare to ring for an appointment.' Nico scowled at his receptionist.

'And?' Josie eyed her moody but darkly handsome boss.

He sighed, his brown eyes agonised. 'I've got to see her but I want some warning. No walk-in visit, OK?'

'Yes, sir.' By Josie's raised eyebrows he guessed she was curious, but Nico held his tongue.

Nico De Burgh returned to his office and strode across the room to stare out of the window into the busy street. When he drew up Frank Treloare's will he'd known it meant facing Patricia again one day, but he hadn't expected it to be so soon. Healthy men in their

4

early fifties weren't supposed to keel over with a heart attack while out in the garden pruning their roses.

He flipped open his mobile and put Helena on speed dial. She answered in an instant with a single, snapped-out 'Yes?'

Ah. He'd committed the cardinal sin of phoning her at work.

'Are you busy tonight? I thought we could go and check out the new wine bar in Rock.'

This wasn't one of their regular twice-a-week date nights but he needed to take his mind off a certain woman from the past. 'I know you're busy getting ready for the Wilson case . . . '

He rubbed at the slight headache building up at his temples as she began to interrogate him like a defence witness.

'Fine — don't worry about it, then. I'll just see you on Saturday, as usual.'

Nico snapped the phone shut and flung it on his desk. Patricia Treloare was already upsetting his hard-won equilibrium and he hadn't yet seen her again.

*   *   *

Annie thrust a mug of tea across the worn pine table, which Tish realised with a jolt was the same table at which she'd sat every day when she was growing up. Tears pressed at her eyes, the unexpected emotion catching her unawares.

'Well — what've you got to say for yourself?'

Her unwilling hostess's aggression threw Tish off-kilter.

'I'm not sure, when I don't even know who you are — or what you're doing here.'

'I'd have thought it was obvious. I'm his widow.' Annie thrust out her left hand, waving the wide gold band in Tish's face.

'Widow?'

'If you'd stayed in touch with your poor father, you'd have known. For years Frank persisted in trying to contact you, but your mother cut him off every time. She said you were better off without him in your life.'

Annie's bitterness left Tish confused. The story her mother had told about her father's neglect was quite different.

'I bumped into your father about five years ago — literally. I was here for the day from Plymouth and he knocked me over, down on the quay.' She tried to smile but it only reached the corners of her mouth. 'To make a long story short, he treated me to lunch and I moved in with him a month later.'

Tish held her silence while her brain struggled to process the woman's bizarre story.

'Last year I got pregnant and he insisted we got married. I wasn't too bothered, but he wanted to do things right. Jamie was born on Christmas Eve.'

A tear leaked from the corner of Annie's right eye. 'Frank adored little Jamie. He always believed he'd failed you, so he felt he'd been given a second chance.' Annie's blue eyes flashed and she smacked her hand on the table. 'He was a damn good father, and he could've been to you too if he'd been allowed.'

Tish needed to escape and do some serious thinking.

'I'd better be going.' She stood and picked up her bag. 'I guess I'll see this Mr De Burgh tomorrow and we'll go from there.' There really wasn't any more to say tonight, she felt.

'Have you got a room booked somewhere?' Annie asked grudgingly, and Tish shook her head. She hadn't thought she'd need one with a whole house at her disposal.

'I suppose you'd better stay, then.' Annie's jaw tightened and she wagged her finger at Tish. 'I'm only offering for his sake, mind. Nothing else.'

Tish tried to be grateful. 'Thank you.'

An awkward silence settled around them and neither made an effort to move. Suddenly the strident wail of a distraught baby pierced the air.

'I thought it was about time.' Annie gave a heavy sigh and dragged herself to her feet. Half way to the door she glanced back at Tish. 'You'd better come and meet your half-brother.'

Half-brother? What the devil would her mother make of this?

'Uh, OK,' she answered.

She followed Annie up the familiar curved staircase, noting the new dark red carpet and fresh white paint.

Annie stopped at the second room along and opened the door, disappearing inside. Tish bit her lip. *My old bedroom.*

From the doorway she watched as Annie reached into the cot and lifted a screaming baby, speaking soothingly. Instantly he went quiet and snuggled into his mother's arms.

The baby lifted his head to peep over Annie's shoulder and Tish let out an involuntary gasp. Tufts of straight, black hair stuck up on his head and his big, light green eyes stared right at her. Her hair and her eyes. After assessing her for a moment, his small, pink mouth turned up in a smile.

Tish's heart clenched. What on earth was she going to do now? This changed everything.

2

'Yes, Mom, I got here fine.' Tish skipped over details of the tortuous drive. She had worse things to discuss than how she'd managed to get here in one piece.

'How long's it goin' to take you to sort out the mess he's left?' She could hear her mum stirring her mid-morning latte.

A lifetime.

'Uh, I'm not sure. There's more to do than I thought.' *Understatement.* 'I'll try to get in to see the solicitor tomorrow and then I'll have a better idea.'

'I still say you're crazy to be there in the first place. You've never shown any interest in going back to Cornwall before now.'

Tish heard her mother's petulance and smiled to herself. 'You didn't exactly encourage me.'

Her mother scoffed. 'Do you blame me?'

Blame? Tish wasn't sure any more. A lot of things she'd thought were facts didn't appear as straightforward as they had done previously. She'd better keep going and get the bad news over with before she completely lost her nerve.

'I've had a couple of surprises already.'

'Don't tell me. They finally got a restaurant selling more than leaden pasties and fish and chips.' Eve Carlisle snickered. 'Is the house a dump? Your father didn't know one end of a paint brush from another and always had his head stuck in a book.'

'It's looking pretty good, actually,' Tish ventured carefully. 'Mom — some-one was staying at the house when I arrived.'

She hesitated, fiddling with the edge of the duvet while she wondered how to say this.

'Patricia Elizabeth! Stop dithering, young lady.'

Gingerly Tish held the phone away from her ear, ready for the outburst in about five seconds.

'Her name's Annie Treloare and she's Dad's widow.'

'What!' Eve shrieked and Tish spoke quickly, preparing herself for the next onslaught.

'He married her last year and they had a baby boy at Christmas. Jamie. He looks just like me, same black hair and pale green eyes, it's uncanny.'

'You gotta be kidding!' Eve shouted, the genteel Southern lady persona she'd cultivated disintegrating in an instant. 'The stupid man. Let me guess. She's a blonde bimbo who conned him by accidentally-on-purpose getting knocked up.'

Tish determined to be honest — one of her biggest virtues, or failings, depending on a person's viewpoint.

'You're wrong, Mom. I'm guessing she's about forty and I got the

13

impression she really loved Dad.'

'Stop right now,' her mother snapped. 'I don't want to hear any more. Do what you have to and get out of there pronto. You can't afford to leave your business for long, anyway, surely?'

Tish's reply stuck in her throat. She hadn't given her Christmas ornament company a thought since Annie Treloare opened the door and shook up her world. They'd have to do without her for a few weeks.

Weeks? She must be losing whatever brains she possessed, especially when the silly season was well underway for getting orders out in readiness for Christmas.

'Don't worry. Sadie will keep things going.' Tish spoke firmly with a confidence she didn't feel, needing to stop her mother's interrogation before it went any further. 'It's only four thirty here but I'm worn out and need to get to bed and crash for a while. I'll talk to you soon, promise.'

She quickly said goodbye and hung

up before her mother could start again. One more call and she'd flop on the narrow, single bed and hopefully sink into oblivion. Five minutes later, she finished talking to the snootiest secretary this side of the pond and had an appointment for the following afternoon. Tish hoped Nico De Burgh wasn't as pretentious as his name suggested. One meeting to sort everything out, and then hopefully she'd be on her way home.

* * *

Nico reached in behind the oversized dictionary on the top shelf of his bookcase, easily despite its height, and removed a small black leather box, its edges rubbed and worn. He normally only gave in and opened it once a year, but his defences were low. He'd see her tomorrow — Josie said she was calling herself Tish Carlisle now, but she was definitely Frank's daughter.

Perching on the edge of the sofa,

Nico placed the box gingerly on the coffee table. He fumbled in his pocket and pulled out a tiny brass key before he could change his mind.

Three pictures, his mother's broken silver necklace, and his father's gold signet ring. All he had left of his past.

Nico took out the picture on the top and smoothed his long, trembling fingers over Patricia's face, laughing at the camera as the wind whipped her long, black hair into a frenzy.

Did you ever love me, or was it only a teenage crush?

The picture gave no hint that the next day she'd be gone from his life with no warning, no explanation.

He couldn't look at the other things today because doing so would wring his heart out, forcing him to feel too much. He'd vowed that never again would he open himself up to such pain.

He slammed shut the lid and checked the lock, walked back over to the bookcase and shoved the box back into its hiding place, where it belonged.

16

* * *

A strange noise sneaked into Tish's tired brain and she stretched out in the bed, almost falling off the edge before catching herself. She groped around on the bedside table for her sleek, silver travel alarm clock — a 1920s Art Deco one she had found in Franklin a few weeks ago and instantly fallen in love with. Six o'clock. Daylight sneaked in through the white, voile curtains and she flopped back onto the pillow, too exhausted to consider getting up.

Suddenly everything came back with a vengeance and she groaned. The crying that had woken her increased to a scream and Annie's light footsteps ran up the stairs. Tish lay still and heard her murmuring soothing words to Jamie — thinking of them as her stepmother and half-brother was just plain weird.

Her stomach rumbled and Tish realised she must have slept straight through dinner time last night. Now her body thought it was midnight and

17

wondered why it had been deprived of food for so long. Slipping out of bed, she pulled on a thin red robe over her Mickey Mouse pyjamas and walked across to open her door.

'Is that you, Tish?' Annie called out from Jamie's room.

It would've been great to sneak downstairs and wake up slowly over a pot of decent coffee, but clearly she didn't have that option.

'Yes,' she replied, trying to sound cheerful.

'I'm sorry if we woke you.' Annie walked along the landing towards her carrying a snuffling baby.

'Don't worry. I need the bathroom, plus I'm ravenous. All screwed up with jet-lag, I guess.'

Annie smiled warmly. 'Come down whenever you're ready. I'll feed this one first, then find us something to eat.'

'If you've got stuff in the fridge I'll happily cook,' Tish offered. 'It's my hobby.'

'Strange — your father loved to cook, too. To me, it's a chore like flossing your teeth or doing the ironing.'

'I don't get to cook as often as I'd like because I'm too busy with my design business.' Tish explained.

'What kind of designs?' Annie asked, suddenly curious.

'I started a Christmas ornament company called Christmas Around the World about five years ago. Our main collection each year focuses on a different country and we've built up a pretty good following.'

'Goodness. I'd no idea.' Annie frowned and sadness pulled at her features. 'I wonder if he knew?' she whispered half to herself.

'Who?'

'Your father, of course,' she retorted.

'Did he have a computer? Was he on the internet a lot?'

Annie nodded and Tish took a steadying breath to calm her churning stomach. 'Then I'm guessing he did. It's not hard to find out about people these days and frankly there's a lot on me out there.'

Yet it hurt to imagine her father tracking her life progress through a search engine.

'He missed out on so much of your life, didn't he?'

Tish couldn't bear to continue this conversation.

'I suppose so. I'm sorry, but I must go. I won't be long.' She turned away and dived into the bathroom.

* * *

'Oh my, that was utterly delicious,' Annie declared with a happy sigh.

'It wasn't anything fancy, only omelette and toast,' Tish protested half-heartedly, pleased to have found an easy way to soften the other woman's attitude towards her.

'Don't be daft. They were all puffy and soft — and you'd done something special to the toast. I'll be enormous if you stay here for very long.'

The hinted-at question was accompanied by a hard stare.

'I'll clean up the dishes and then get a shower, if that's OK with you?' Tish changed the subject. Annie must be worried about her future and Jamie's but was too proud to ask outright, and Tish couldn't reassure her until she'd met the solicitor.

'Of course.'

'I've got an appointment in Truro at two this afternoon with Mr De Burgh, but I'm planning to pop in early and have a wander around to see what it's like these days. I hear you've a lot of charity shops and I'm into vintage clothes.'

'I'd noticed.' Annie smiled, scanning Tish's carefully chosen psychedelic mini-dress and knee-high white boots.

'I was in a Sixties mood this morning.'

'It's certainly different,' Annie conceded. 'If I tried it, I'd look as if I'd dragged out a load of old clothes from my mother's wardrobe. Works on you, though.'

'Thanks. I got into the whole fashion

thing at art school and I guess I enjoy being outside the box.'

She didn't share the fact that her offbeat style had started as a form of protection when she didn't fit in anyway and was determined to show she didn't care.

Annie threw her a shrewd glance but didn't say any more.

'Off you go and see to Jamie,' Tish insisted and gratefully the older woman left her visitor to clear the breakfast things.

This was a hundred times harder than she'd expected. It was no longer a question of simply sorting through her father's papers, getting rid of his old clothes and signing a few legal papers before running off back to Nashville.

Tish gathered up the dirty dishes from the table and moved them over to the counter, ready to be washed. Putting order back into the kitchen would help steady her down. It always worked in Nashville — so there was

22

no reason why it shouldn't work in Cornwall, too.

Mr Nico De Burgh would follow her instructions later, and everyone would be happy.

3

'Miss Carlisle is here to see you, sir,' Josie announced. Nico kept his back to the door for another few seconds and swallowed hard to moisten his dry throat, only then daring to turn around.

'Good afternoon, Miss Carlisle. Do come in and take a seat.'

He steeled himself not to show any obvious reaction beyond a bland half-smile. Inside he was seventeen again and trying to appear cool while his heart thumped and his palms sweated.

'Nick? Nick Penwarren? I don't believe it.' She broke into a glorious smile, zeroing in all his attention on her glossy, red lips.

She threw herself at Nico, almost knocking him off his feet, and tightened her long arms around his neck. A swirl of ebony hair brushed his face and he was surrounded by a lush scent, something spicy and teasing. Nico's body tightened involuntarily and he gently disentangled her, taking a step back before he embarrassed them both.

A tiny frown marred her beautiful face. 'What's up? Don't even try to say you've forgotten me. I won't believe you.'

Her light, honeyed drawl took him by surprise, although it shouldn't have done. Fourteen years was a long time.

Forgotten you? Are you out of your mind?

'What's with the name thing? And all this?' She stepped back and gestured around at his office. 'I thought you'd be a world-renowned artist by now. Don't tell me you gave up on your plans? Of all the jobs I could never imagine you doing, this tops the list.'

The curious pale green eyes which had haunted his dreams for years pierced right through him and Nico stumbled over his reply. The truth wasn't an option.

'Goodness, Patricia, that was nothing more than a childish fantasy. Why don't you take a seat and we'll talk?' He needed her at least a desk width away to keep himself in check.

Tish's deep, warm laugh filled the room. 'No one calls me Patricia these days, it's too stuffy and English — something I've got far away from being, unlike you. Hell, Nick, you're very pompous these days. Maybe I should tell your prim receptionist about the night on the beach when we skinny-dipped and smoked pot.' Her eyes flashed with mischief.

'For God's sake . . . keep your voice down.' Nico ached to rip his tie off and cool his overheated blood.

'Ok, I will if you stop acting like you don't know me,' she challenged.

'I *knew* you, many years ago. It's not the same thing. How about we get down to the business in hand?'

'Whatever. I'll play along for now, but just so we're clear — I didn't choose to leave, and I did write you multiple letters. You're the one who never wrote back.'

The quiet words sliced through him, but he refused to rise to her bait. There was a lot he could tell Miss Tish Carlisle about what her leaving did to him, but it wasn't up for discussion. It never would be, if he had his way.

'Ok, I get the hint.' Tish chose the seat nearest his desk, arranging herself so that he was forced to look directly at her. As she crossed her legs Nico caught a glimpse of smooth, tanned thigh above the shiny, white boots as her wildly-coloured mini dress rose threateningly high. Along with his blood pressure.

'At least explain the Nico De Burgh name thing.'

He wished she'd let it go, but persistence was always one of her dubious charms.

'There's no great mystery. I simply reverted to my birth name. You knew I came from Sicily to live with the

Penwarrens because of . . . family circumstances. I took their name to fit in easier at school. Later on it wasn't necessary any more.'

'I guess.' She swept him with her appraising gaze and his skin prickled with a film of sweat. 'Let's get this over with.'

'I've got your father's will here.' He picked the document up from his desk and hesitated. 'Have you been to the Beach Road house yet?'

'Yeah, I went straight there when I arrived yesterday.' The corners of her generous mouth turned up in a faint smile. 'What you're really asking is, have I discovered his second family? Being a typical circumspect lawyer, of course you won't spell it out as frankly. I didn't know about Annie and Jamie and it was a shock, but we're kind of OK today. She felt sorry enough to let me stay last night. Obviously you know her?'

He nodded, toying with his silver pen and choosing his words with care.

'Yes, I've had some dealings with Mrs Treloare. I'm not betraying a confidence by telling you she contacted me after your father's death wanting to know where she stood.'

'Why didn't he change his will after Jamie was born?'

'I suggested it, but like many people he thought he had plenty of time.' Nico leaned forward slightly and caught another hint of her tantalising perfume. The girl he'd known so long ago used plain soap and occasionally pinched her father's cologne.

'Unfortunately he was wrong.' His words brought an instant film of tears to her pretty eyes and he ached to wipe them away.

'I need to put things right,' she stated with a firmness which took him aback. 'I want you to put the house in trust for Jamie and give Annie a generous allowance to take care of them both.'

Nico hated to put a damper on her generous offer.

'I'm sorry, but it's out of the question.'

'Why?' She nibbled at her lip, smudging the bright red.

'Your father was in financial difficulties when he died. He'd remortgaged the house and fallen behind with the payments. Here's the foreclosure note from the bank.' He pushed a sheet of legal paper across the desk, hating to be the cause of her distress. 'The first of next month it'll belong to the bank.' Nico rested his shaky hands on the antique leather-topped desk.

'Does Annie know about this?' Tish murmured, quickly scanning the page.

'Your father tried to keep from her how bad things were, but she's not stupid and suspects something is wrong.'

'What happened for things to get so bad?'

'Frank lost his teaching job when there were cutbacks. He picked up some part-time work but it wasn't enough, then Jamie arrived and, well . . . ' Nico's voice trailed away and he couldn't quite meet her questioning eyes.

'I'm guessing he tried to hold onto the house for my sake as well as his new family?'

'I advised him to declare bankruptcy and move into rented accommodation.' He skirted around giving a direct answer.

'He didn't want me to come home and discover the house sold, did he?' she persisted and he gave in.

'No. Are you satisfied now?'

'Honesty is the best way. I don't pussy-foot around these days. I'm not the ditzy teenager you remember.'

'So I've noticed,' he quipped.

'I'm glad you haven't completely lost your sense of humour. I improved your English and trained you to love *Fawlty Towers* and *Monty Python* at the same time, didn't I?' Tish smirked at the memories.

He gave a small nod, not daring to say any more.

'How much are we talking about for the house?'

He wasn't sorry she had changed the subject; he avoided the past like the plague. He glanced at the bank letter again. 'Just under four hundred thousand.'

'Ok. That's not a problem.'

'I'm sorry?' He decided he must have misheard.

'I'll pay it off, and then we'll follow through on my earlier suggestions.'

'Tish, do you understand how much it is in dollars?'

Maths was never her strong subject; he'd helped her with enough algebra homework in his time.

She sprang out of the chair, slammed her hands down on the desk and leaned in, inches away from his face. Nico struggled not to stare at the lush, heaving breasts she certainly didn't have fourteen years ago.

'Don't patronise me.'

Nico pressed further back in the chair for his own sanity. Her explosive anger aroused him beyond all common sense, but he must remember that he was her solicitor and nothing more.

'I apologise. I didn't mean to offend you, but surely you can't afford it?'

Tish's raunchy laughter filled the room and hit him direct in the stomach. 'You don't have a clue. I could buy the house several times over and never miss the money.'

She flung herself back down in the chair and her glossy ebony hair fell back into place around her shoulders. 'Go on, ask me. You know you want to,' she challenged, glancing up through the long, black lashes sweeping her porcelain-clear skin.

He didn't reply. She'd never been able to keep a secret, so he knew he wouldn't have to wait long.

'Remember I was always drawing?'

'Yes, especially in class when you were supposed to be studying.' A brief rumbling laugh broke out of him and as their eyes met, the breath caught in his throat. Pure desire shot through his gut and it took all his self-control to sit still. He wanted to yank her up to standing, press himself into her soft curves and kiss her senseless — just for starters.

'Nick. I — '

Hearing her say his old name brought him back to where they were, and he struggled to steady himself. 'You were explaining what you do these days.'

'Sure.' Her soft, breathy voice aroused him yet further and he squirmed in the chair. If he had to stand right now, he wouldn't be able to hide from her just how turned on she had made him. 'I've got a very successful Christmas ornament company,' she went on.

'Can you make a living selling those things?' He couldn't hide his amazement.

Tish's brilliant smile returned, showing off her white, even teeth. 'Mine are unique, one-offs from all around the world, and others are personally designed for my customers. Trust me, I can easily afford to do this. But there's one condition.'

'Go on.'

'Annie can't know. She's proud, and will go ape if she finds out. I'm sure you're clever enough to work out a way to do this. Get it all put together and I'll sign whatever's necessary.'

'I'll need your financial details for the bank and somehow come up with a good story to tell Mrs Treloare.'

'How about we brainstorm over dinner later?'

He winced as she laid down the challenge. *No. Bad idea.*

'I don't socialise with clients.'

'I'll give in and call you Nico, but don't you ever call me a mere client again.' Her low, deadly words sliced through his skin, reducing him to an ill-mannered teenage boy again.

'I'm sorry. How about I pick you up at eight and we go to the Blue Anchor?'

'Sure we're old enough? Old man Taylor threw us out the last time we tried.' Her wicked grin drew one from him too; she'd always known how to poke holes in his stiff, protective shell.

'I think we might get away with it.'

'Ok, then, it's a date.'

He almost replied, *no it isn't*, but it'd sound churlish. Tish stood and he automatically did the same.

'I'd better be going,' she announced regretfully. He stepped out around the desk and stood in front of her.

'I'll see you later.' Nico lifted his hand close to her cheek and naked anticipation flared in her eyes. He pushed his arm firmly back to his side.

'Oh, you will indeed.' Out of nowhere Tish pressed a brief kiss against his cheek and her lips seared his skin. 'Until later.'

Nico watched her leave his office, her slim hips swaying and the short dress tightening around her cute backside. A tight knot of tension ran through his shoulders, settled in his groin. Now he had tonight to get through . . . and he only had a limited amount of self-control.

4

Tish turned her key in the lock and stepped into the hall, sensing the empty house wrap around her. Good.

She hadn't forgotten which stairs creaked — she'd made use of the skill often enough to sneak out and meet Nick. Nico. The last person she'd expected to see again, and the one who brought everything rushing back — things she'd rather forget.

For a minute she hesitated outside her father's old study before she dared to open the door . . . Strong mints, pipe tobacco and joss sticks, the three smells she associated with him, hit her so hard that she was compelled to seize hold of the door frame to stay upright.

Tish made herself step inside and her gaze immediately homed in on the window seat, still covered in the same worn green velvet. She picked her way around the piles of books scattered on the floor and sat down. She held back the tears pressing at her eyes, and bent down to pull out the drawer beneath her legs. He had kept her favourite books there, and spent hours reading to her until her mother told them both off.

She didn't recognise the small blue book she pulled out, but flipping it open she immediately recognised her father's spidery writing.

'A diary. You kept a diary?' Tish dug around some more and found a whole pile of similar notebooks — all with the year embossed in gold on the front.

'What do you think you're doing?' Annie's sharp voice from the doorway startled Tish.

'You said it was alright for me to look through Dad's things and see if there was anything I wanted.' She wasn't going to be treated like a naughty child by this unknown woman.

Annie snatched the book from Tish's hand and clutched it to her chest. 'I didn't mean those.'

Tish bit the edge of her tongue, tasting blood.

'Those are private. He told me to burn them if anything happened to him, but . . . I couldn't.' Annie's blue eyes shone with unshed tears.

'I'm sorry. Of course I'll respect your wishes, but it'd be great if you'd reconsider.' Tish's brain raced through different options, searching for the right one to change Annie's mind. 'I'd like to know him better,' she said simply. 'Have you read them?'

Annie shook her head. 'I came in once when he was writing and it was the only time he ever got angry at me.'

'Would you like to know what's in there?' Tish probed. She wasn't a woman to leave things alone; her mother often called her aggravating, though she considered herself deter-mined.

'Well, Jamie's taking a nap,' Annie said with a sly half-smile.

Tish took it as permission and began sorting the books into date order, picking out the oldest one to start with. Annie selected another and sat down at her late husband's old oak desk, holding the diary with the tips of her fingers as if it might explode. They began to read, their quiet breathing the only sounds in the room.

★ ★ ★

Nico threw his jacket on the back of the sofa and followed it with his tie. He was a fool. What had possessed him to agree to Tish's dinner invitation? He tried to rationalise it but in his gut, he knew it had simply been the sight and smell of her filling his office, the silky black hair grazing her shoulders and her sparkling sea-green eyes laughing and setting his body on fire. She'd been pretty at sixteen, but now she was flat out beautiful. To keep his promise to his family might be impossible.

He seized the grappa bottle and poured out a large measure, sinking it in one long swallow.

Damn you, Tish. Why did you have to come back?

His foster father had asked only one thing of him, and for a very good reason. At the time, it had been an easy promise to make because seeing Tish again was as likely as him going to Mars. Now everything had changed.

Nico took his glass back to the kitchen, rinsed it out and set it on the draining board to dry. He'd go upstairs and change his clothes, pick up Tish and simply behave like an old friend.

He laughed out loud and was sure the room laughed back. Who was he kidding?

★   ★   ★

Tish rubbed at the back of her stiff neck. 'Nothing very interesting so far. How about you?'

Annie shook her head. 'No. It's mainly lists of books he'd read and his own poems. There's nothing earth-shattering so I can't imagine why he

41

wanted them destroyed.'

'I'm quitting now and I'll read some more tomorrow. I need to get start getting ready for my hot date,' Tish jested.

'Hot date?' Annie grinned in spite of herself. 'You've only been here a day. How did you manage that?'

'I'm exaggerating a tad. Dad's esteemed solicitor is taking me to dinner.'

'Mr De Burgh? Does the glamorous Helena know?'

'Helena?' Surely he didn't have a wife and six children he'd forgotten to mention?

'His girlfriend, Helena Worthington. She's a barrister in the Crown Court, very elegant and brainy. I gather they've been together for years with no hint of wedding bells. All the women around here swoon over his good looks and his Italian accent, but he never takes the bait. They reckon he's commitment-phobic and Helena's a cold fish — a perfect match, I'd say.' Annie smirked.

'I think there's a smouldering volcano under his Armani exterior which only needs the right trigger to erupt.'

Aaagh — she should have guessed a gorgeous man like Nico would be spoken for, no matter how serious and reserved he appeared these days.

'It's just dinner. We're old friends. He was the first boy I kissed.' *And the first and last I fell in love with.* 'I do believe I need to find something interesting to wear.'

Annie's eyes gleamed. 'Put on something sexy. He needs shaking up.'

Tish pondered for a second. 'How about the Seventies disco thing? Tight white trousers, a sparkly top and platform heels?'

'Should make him look.' Annie stood up. 'I'd better go and check on Jamie.'

'Don't wait up for me,' Tish teased, then quickly shook her head. 'I'm only joking.'

'Enjoy yourself. I might read another volume before bed.' Annie picked up the next diary.

'I'll look forward to hearing more of Dad's exciting stories later.' Tish ran from the room, grinning as she went.

★ ★ ★

Tish watched the play of emotions fighting for control of Nico's face as she opened the front door. His dark, liquid brown gaze swept down over her and his jaw tightened perceptibly.

'Had a good look? You've seen it all before.' She smirked and poked a finger in the middle of his chest, hitting a wall of solid muscle. A rush of heat made her cheeks burn.

He cleared his throat. 'We'd better go.'

'What's the rush? Is the Blue Anchor going to close in the next thirty minutes?'

'Do you want dinner or not?' Nico snapped, his accent thickening.

'Don't be such a dreary old spoil-sport.' She stepped out of the house and closed the door behind her. 'Is that your car?' The old blue Volvo parked on the side of the road wasn't what she'd envisioned.

'What's wrong with it?'

'I can't imagine any self-respecting Sicilian man driving such a staid car.'

His eyes narrowed. 'I've lived here a long time. Plus I'm only a humble solicitor — not one of the American millionaires you no doubt hang around with on a regular basis.'

Tish kept quiet. She doubted many other Cornish lawyers wore Armani, the latest designs straight off this year's catwalk. There'd always been more to Nico than met the eye.

She trailed a fingernail along his arm. 'I'm one too, remember — and yes, I mean millionaire as well as American.'

'Is there really so much money in Christmas ornaments?'

'For your information, I'm not merely selling a few Christmas balls in the local shops. Christmas Around the World has international customers — and I built it all up myself.' Tish hated to brag, but his ironic jibe irritated her.

'Sorry, Pat . . . I mean, Tish. I didn't intend to offend you.' A polite façade slipped back across his handsome face, covering the flash of desire she'd caught sight of a few minutes earlier.

Tish opened the car door and slid in before he could remember his manners. 'Come on, let's go. I'm starving.'

Nico didn't reply and walked around to get in the driver's side. He folded his long legs into the seat, stuck his key in the ignition and kept his eyes turned away.

'Did Helena approve our little expedition tonight?' She examined her fingernails, pleased with the effect of the new silver glitter polish she'd experimented with.

He tightened his grip on the steering wheel and she tried hard not to stare at his tempting muscular arms, imagining the effect they could have on her if he put them to good use.

'I assume Annie's been gossiping?'

'If you want to call it that. You gonna answer me?'

'We're not possessive of each other. It's not that sort of relationship,' he growled.

'Oh, come on. Don't spout that old line.' The fierce glare he flung in her direction took Tish's breath away. Boy, she'd like to tame Nico De Burgh. The gangly teenage boy she'd befriended at eleven and fallen in love with at fifteen was long gone, replaced by the hottest man she'd seen in years. She'd been too consumed by work recently to have any time for a personal life, but a little flirtation couldn't hurt. And he clearly needed to unwind a little, she reasoned.

'You're simply an old friend, so there's no reason for her to be concerned,' he declared in a flat, expressionless voice.

Tish leaned up against his broad shoulder and blew gently on the side of his neck. 'Are you sure?' She fought back the temptation to rub her fingers along the dark stubble shading his rigid jaw line.

'Absolutely. Behave yourself, Tish.' He sounded exasperated, but she wasn't ready to play nice.

'Are you positive you want me to?' She dragged one nail slowly along his bare lower arm, teasing the soft dark hairs until she reached the sleeve of his forest-green polo shirt. There was nothing remotely English about his Mediterranean looks, nor the way he dressed. The shirt and dark jeans were both top quality and fitted perfectly, showing off his lean, fit body. Exactly what she liked to tangle with under the sheets, when she had the chance.

Sometimes you have to make your own chances, girl.

Nico shoved her hand away. 'Forget it,' he rasped and she suppressed a giggle, knowing she'd wriggled under his skin.

The more stern and serious he became, the more she wanted to break through his buttoned up façade. Underneath this cool quasi-Englishman lay the hot-tempered boy who'd set her on fire with a single kiss. But for now, she'd crank it down and lull him into thinking he'd put her in her place.

'I'm sorry. My brain must still be affected by jet-lag. I really want to know what you've been up to since I left, so let's have a fun evening catching up.' She plastered on an open, ingenuous smile, but his instant scowl said he wasn't fooled.

'We're here.' He pulled into an empty parking space on the street and turned off the engine.

'Great.' Tish waited as he got out to walk around the car. He opened her door and out of the corner of her eye she caught him sneak a look at her legs as she stepped out onto the pavement. Pavement — funny, she hadn't called it anything but a sidewalk in years.

This promised to be the most interesting evening she'd had in a long time. If she didn't manage at least a searing kiss with her old boyfriend by the end of the evening, her powers were surely failing. Her blood tingled at the thought of cracking Nico De Burgh's shell.

5

Tish poked her fork around the plate and peered at the food. 'What's wrong?' Nico asked. 'Not up to your standards?'

'I thought the menu said the scampi came with a salad. I'd hardly call one lettuce leaf and two slices of cucumber a salad.'

Nico fought against laughing, because the minute he let his guard down he'd be in trouble. 'Remember you're in the Blue Anchor where salads are suspect and anyone who asks for any sort of fancy dressing instead of salad cream must be foreign.' He dug back into his fish and chips, drenched in vinegar and sprinkled with an unhealthy helping of salt.

'No more complaints. Promise.' She flashed a brilliant smile and everything from her clear, creamy skin to her glossy red mouth glowed. He sighed, wishing Frank Treloare hadn't died and put him in this position.

'You've nearly finished yours, so it can't be bad.'

'It's good, thank you,' he replied politely and shut down the conversation, determined to get their business out of the way so that he could take her home and escape. 'Let's discuss your plan regarding the Beach Road house. By the way, I suggest you don't speak too loud — the village gossips would love to spread this juicy piece of news around.'

Tish slid along the wooden bench and pressed her hip up against his. 'Are you saying I'm loud?' she mouthed into his ear. 'How ungentlemanly of you.'

If she kept up this barrage of suggestive remarks, his thin string of self-control would snap and hit him on the rebound.

'Don't twist my words. You know exactly what I mean. For goodness' sake, stop acting like a vamp. You aren't Marilyn Monroe.' *You're far worse.*

'OK, OK. Back to business.' She eased away and plastered an apologetic smile on her face. 'Annie knows Dad left me the house, so we have to find a way to let her and Jamie stay there without her knowing I paid for it in the first place.'

He laid down his knife and fork on the empty plate. Dining here was a welcome relief from the fancy places Helena preferred, which served minute portions of organic vegetables and a sliver of meat accompanied by a glass or two of the finest wine. Cod and chips washed down with a pint of Tribute ale was hard to beat.

Nico leaned back in the chair and struggled to keep his brain on track. Tish's nearness and the waft of warm, spicy perfume tickling his senses made it damn near impossible.

'Annie's not a stupid woman. She must've guessed it's not yours to give freely, even if she'd accept the offer. We can't spin a ridiculous tale about previously unknown investments or a recently discovered diamond necklace.

Your father kept hoping something would turn up before things got this bad.'

The next words slipped out before he could stop them. 'You did, of course — just not in time.'

She blanched, her skin changing from rich cream to chalk white in a second.

'Oh — I'm sorry, Tish. I didn't mean . . . '

'It's alright,' she stammered and glanced away.

'No, it's not. The last thing I intended was to hurt you.'

She pinned him with a bright, defiant smile, her pale eyes shiny with tears. 'I told you it was alright and I meant it. I know I should've come before and I've already had the same lecture from Annie. As soon as this is all sorted, I'll be out of your hair and it'll be a cold day in hell before I return to Cornwall.'

She snatched up her wine glass and drained the deep, red liquid in one gulp. 'You can get me another drink and then take me back to Beach

Road. We're done.'

'But the plan . . . '

'We'll think about it on our own, then share ideas at your office or over the phone. I guess I hoped we could have a pleasant enough evening together, but boy, was I wrong.' Tish glared at Nico, daring him to say any more.

He gave a curt nod and went up to the bar, returning with another large glass of merlot. Setting it down in front of her, he sat at the far end of the bench, giving her a wide berth.

'It's alright,' she observed tartly. 'I'm not going to either burst into tears or smack you.'

He grimaced. 'Well, you have done both in the past.'

'Still got the scars, have you?'

You don't have a clue. 'Time heals all wounds.'

'You don't really believe that crap, do you?'

For a second he was tempted to be honest, but dropped his eyes to his empty glass.

'Finish your drink and we'll go,' he muttered.

'Smooth, aren't you? Do you treat Helena this way?'

Nico refused to rise to her taunts. 'She's not up for discussion.'

'I didn't think she would be.' Tish swallowed the rest of her wine and thumped the glass down so hard that it rocked unsteadily when she let go. 'I'm ready.' She jumped up and her curtain of silky hair swung temptingly around before it settled back down around her shoulders.

He itched to cradle her face in his hands and kiss the combativeness away. Instead he sucked in a deep breath, stood up and slid a bland expression back on his face. 'Right.' He strode towards the door without checking to see if she followed.

* * *

Nico cursed as he stepped outside the pub and spotted his car. 'Damn vandals. Haven't they anything better to do?' He stomped all around the vehicle, shouting every rough Italian curse word he knew. 'All four tyres slashed. Great. What a perfect end to the evening.'

'Screwed up like the rest of the night, isn't it?' Tish's sultry drawl teased over his shoulder.

'Sorry. I shouldn't have gone off that way. I need to call the police and a recovery truck.' He ought to push away the comforting hand she rested on his arm, but made no move to do so. 'Why don't I call you a taxi so you won't have to wait around while I deal with all this hassle?'

'We came on an evening out together, and I'll stay to the bitter end.' She poked his ribs and grinned. 'If only to bug you.'

'Fine — it's your choice.' Nico dared not respond to her humour, something else about her he hadn't allowed himself to miss. For his own sanity he walked away and started to make his calls. After a fruitless discussion with the police, who only told him to fill out a report in the morning, he slammed the phone shut. Turning back around he saw Tish sprawled comfortably on the old wood bench outside the pub.

'Come and join me, you might as well.' She made room for him, crossed her long legs and pulled down the silver top, its sequins glittering in the moonlight and clinging to curves he'd fought to ignore all evening. 'I won't bite,' she teased, pretending to gnash her lovely white teeth.

You going to give me that in writing? 'Thanks.'

'Lovely, isn't it? I've missed this.' She made room for him to sit down and stared across the road at the small harbour spread out in front of them. Nico's strained body went into overdrive from trying to ignore her tempting scent and the spreading warmth from her firm thigh pressed up against his leg. Concentrating on the setting sun was next to impossible, so he tried desperately to make rational conversation.

'I understand. I moved away for several years but something drew me back.'

'Where did you go?'

'To university in London, and afterwards I spent several years working in Manchester. That's where I met Helena. We were the only non-Northerners in our law office.' His voice trailed away. How come Tish always made him say more than he intended? She'd done it as a young girl, and now he appeared to be as vulnerable to her probing as ever.

'I guess you got into the habit of being with her?' She fixed her curious gaze on him and at last he reached out to touch her cheek, tempted beyond reason by her smooth, perfect skin. 'It's easy to do. My last boyfriend . . . ' Her eyes widened as he stroked gently down to rest at the hollow at the base of her throat.

Under his teasing fingers, her pulse

raced and his body tightened with anticipation. He'd have to kiss her before he self-combusted on the spot.

'Mr De Burgh?' A burly tow-truck driver in worn overalls stood by his car and Nico pulled himself together, giving silent thanks for the interruption.

'You want it taken over to Haskins — that right?'

He nodded and took his car key off the ring, passing it over.

'Do you need a lift anywhere, mate? I can fit you both in,' the man offered with a cheery smile.

'No, thanks. I live nearby. I'll get out my other car to take the lady home. Cheers.'

'No prob. I'll pop your key in Haskins' drop box and you can contact them in the morning.' The man walked back into the street and got busy with the car.

'So I get to see your humble abode. What an unexpected treat.' Tish laughed, her eyes sparkling with mischief.

Nico scraped around in his brain for

a plausible excuse. His idea was to get his Alfa Romeo out of the garage and take her back to Beach Road, but plainly she had other ideas. Years ago he'd come up against the immovable force of the old Patricia Treloare; the new improved version was ten times worse.

He sighed. How on earth would he get out of this one?

6

Tish could barely suppress her glee. Poor Nico resembled a man sentenced to the guillotine. She slipped her hand through his arm and tightened her hold before he could pull away. 'Lead on, Sir Lancelot. Whisk the Lady Guinevere off to your castle.'

A dark red flush crept up his neck and his face turned to stone. He'd always been ridiculously easy to tease. She'd made the cute, sullen boy with the adorable accent her project the April she turned fifteen, and by the time summer was over he was eating out of her hand.

'For pity's sake, Tish. We're only going to get my car.'

'Don't be a spoilsport. As a gentleman I'm sure you'll at least ask me in for coffee.' By his dark-eyed glare Tish guessed that was all he intended giving her. She'd see about that.

He took off at a brisk walk, and steered them away from the harbour before turning down the first narrow side street. Tish's silver platform shoes wobbled over the rough cobblestones and she could barely keep up with his long-legged stride. They didn't speak, which gave her a chance to study him again without him throwing a fit. He really was a delectable specimen of manhood. Her mouth watered, imagining what she could do to him.

'Have you decided I'm not a monster?' Nico's smooth, low voice held a hint of a laughter.

'What do you mean?'

'Your eyes have bored into me for the last couple of minutes as though you were trying to decide if I was Jack the Ripper reincarnated.'

It was a good job he couldn't read her mind as well as he thought. She'd push another button and see his reaction.

'I wondered if the brooding, lost boy

I remember was still inside somewhere.'

He jerked to a halt and she almost tripped over. Nico planted his large, muscular hands on her shoulders to steady her. His liquid brown eyes bored into her and a shot of pure desire snaked through Tish's body, making it hard to breathe.

'So what did you decide?' he demanded.

'Oh, he's there.' She struggled to keep her voice level. 'The surface is smooth and confident these days, but I bet I could still wring you out if I put my mind to it.'

Swiftly he closed the gap between them and slid his hands up either side of her face. The press of his fingers made her skin tighten all over.

'You're convinced you know everything about me but you haven't a clue. There's so much I could show you, tesoro, darling, Tish.' He was breathing hard.

The hint of Italian finished her off, as it had done when she was a girl.

'Why don't we start with your house?' She stepped backwards, forcing him to drop his hands to his sides.

'It's around the corner,' he said politely, the angles of his face razor-sharp in the shadowed light. She didn't risk taking his arm this time, taken aback by her violent reaction to his one brief touch.

They walked silently, side by side, until he stopped outside a small cottage on the end of a row of typical old fishermen's houses. Illuminated brass lamps on either side of the dark blue door showed up the pale blue walls and white-painted windows.

'It's not at all what I expected.' She stood back and admired the house, noticing the well-cared for hanging baskets overflowing with velvety red pansies. 'I thought the new Nico would own a super-modern apartment gleaming with stainless steel and black leather.'

He gave an easy shrug. 'I've always preferred old places.'

Unlocking the door, he pushed it open, then stood back for her to step in first.

*   *   *

Nico closed the door behind them before he turned to face her again, needing the extra few seconds to collect himself. 'Would you prefer coffee or a drink?'

'Coffee's great. Annie's been pouring tea down me non-stop since I arrived,' she answered with a wry smile.

He headed into the narrow galley-style kitchen, aware she must be following as her sultry perfume filled the small room.

'Very nice. I'm guessing by all this that you like to cook?' Tish began to poke around, opening the oven and giving his heavy copper-bottomed saucepans on display an approving nod.

'Yes, I do. I ripped out all the old cupboards and appliances and tried to maximize the limited space.' This was

66

safer ground, he could do this. 'How about you?'

She stepped over to the counter and examined his new stainless steel blender. 'I love to, whenever I have time. I've had a new Viking range installed but I haven't got to use it much yet. You'll have to cook for me one day.'

'Maybe.' Nico filled up the coffee pot and turned it on. 'It'll be a few minutes. Do you want to see around the place?'

'Sure thing.' Tish rubbed at one of her ankles. 'Do you mind if I take my shoes off? These weren't designed for tottering around on cobblestones.'

'Go ahead.' She bent over to loosen the straps and he couldn't drag his gaze from the inches of exposed skin between her sparkly top and the tight, white trousers. He shoved his hands into his pockets out of the way of temptation. She pushed the offending shoes under the table and straightened back up.

'Lead the way.' Her broad smile threatened to melt his resolve, and swiftly he stepped back into the other room out of its range.

'I'm sure you remember what these houses were like originally. I knocked the two rooms into one to give the illusion of more space. It took ages to find a small enough sofa to fit both the room and my long legs — they still hang off the end.' Her encouraging nod made him carry on. 'I stripped the wood floor myself and used the dark stain because I feel the modern pine finish most people choose was wrong for this place.'

'I love it, and these rugs are perfect.' She pointed to the soft red and cream patterned rugs he'd scoured Cornwall to find, ending up at an artisan weaver in St Ives. 'It's really charming. Did Helena help with the decorating?'

He shook his head. 'No, it's all my doing, for good or ill.' He didn't add the fact that Helena disliked his house because it wasn't impressive enough for her tastes.

'You like your gadgets.' With a laugh

she gestured towards the large flat screen TV and sound system against the wall.

'Hey, I'm a man, what can I say?'

Their eyes met, and for several long seconds he couldn't breathe. How would she react if he pulled her into his arms and kissed her senseless? No! No! Nico ordered his painfully aroused body to calm down before she noticed and mocked him.

She broke their gaze and glanced around the room. 'I love all your artwork.'

'They're all by local artists. Helena thinks there are too many, but . . . ' His voice trailed away, not wanting to go where the conversation was headed.

'No, she's wrong about that — they're perfect.' She sounded irate on his behalf, which gave him an unexpected kick.

He headed towards the stairs, wanting to get this over with and her out of here before he cracked.

'After you.' Nico gestured for her to

go ahead of him and didn't resist the natural urge to check out her neat, curvy backside all the way up. At the top, she glanced back over her shoulder and caught him out. A rush of heat swept up his neck as her lips curled into a teasing smile.

'Naughty, naughty.' She wagged her finger and laughed.

He refused to respond and passing her on the top step, flung open the first door. 'Bathroom.' She poked her head in and checked it out. He walked right past the next door, not wishing to open the can of worms that would be entailed by showing her that room. 'That's the guest bedroom.' He crossed the narrow hall and opened the only other door. 'This is my room.'

Tish stepped inside and a quick sweep of the room confirmed her fear. He was a neat freak. The large brass bed with its immaculate sapphire-blue duvet and regimentally arranged pillows blended well with the dark wood floor. She wiggled her bare toes in the thick cream rug under her feet, having instant wicked thoughts about what it would feel like against bare skin. Plain wooden blinds at the window proclaimed this a man's room, simple and straightforward, with nothing unnecessary to soften the effect.

It was the complete opposite of her own unco-ordinated mishmash of pillows, stuffed animals and souvenirs from her travels. Her bedside table held toppling piles of cookery books, romances and her secret vice — horror stories. Nico's contrasting neat stack of books contained serious biographies and military fiction, all arranged in alphabetical order.

'It's very . . . '

'Plain. I know. Most men just want a comfortable bed and a decent light for reading. Women always go for . . . *stuff*.'

She threw up her hands in fake surrender. 'Guilty as charged, I'm afraid.'

Nico seized hold of her hands and his severe features softened into a teasing smile. The transformation sent a rush of pure desire sweeping through right to her core. She wanted him. It was that simple.

'Tish.' The hoarse rasp of his voice encouraged her and she loosened her hands to slide them around his neck, pulling him down to her. The second his firm lips touched hers, she sighed in ecstasy at the remembered taste. Nico's tongue teased insistently and she softened, opening to his exploration.

'So sweet.' His large, sure hands lingered at her waist then cupped her rear, pressing her hard up against his body. Nico nestled his rigid arousal against her, rhythmically pulsing and driving her mad with the need for him to be buried deep inside her. The sensations sent her swirling back in time.

At their last school dance he'd swept her into a slow number and, to the hypnotic beat of the music, moved closer until they touched in this same, intimate way. She'd never felt a boy that way before, her limited knowledge coming from her mother's romance novels and giggling conversations with her girlfriends. It had scared her until he'd smiled and reassured her he'd never hurt her or do anything she wasn't ready for.

He deepened the kiss, sending her senses reeling. Tish returned his passion, beat for beat.

'Sei cosi bella, you're so beautiful,' he murmured against her throat, nipping and teasing with his teeth. 'You were always lovely but now I don't have the words.'

Nico slid one hand under the hem of her sequined top, stroking her overheated skin, and she prayed he wouldn't stop. He reached around her back and flipped open her bra, flashing a wicked smile and setting her heart on fire.

'Forget words, just touch me,' she whispered.

'Lift your arms,' he growled and she obeyed. In one swift move he peeled off her top and the bra with it, tossing them to the floor. Nico's sinful, dark eyes burned a path in her skin as he focused on her breasts, an appreciative groan coming from the back of his throat. He bent over, seizing one sensitive tip in his mouth, nipping and sucking, swirling his tongue in teasing circles until all the strength left her body. His body ground into her relentlessly and she writhed against him. 'Tell me now if you want me to stop, cara, dear, Tish.'

'Never! Oh, Nico, it was always you. Don't wait any longer.'

Suddenly his body stilled and he stepped back away from her so fast that she almost lost her balance.

'Hell!' Horror suffused his face. 'My God, Tish, I'm so sorry. I don't know what came over me.' His skin turned pale under his tan, and bile rose in his throat. 'Go! Go, Tish — please.'

Tish glared right back and stood her ground. 'What's wrong? You want me as much as I want you. Who're you trying to fool?'

'Myself,' he whispered gruffly. 'I can't explain. I'm sorry.'

'You will one day, whether you like it or not.' She grabbed her clothes and quickly got dressed. 'This isn't the end, Nico. Some things just are, and this is one of them.'

Without another word she ran back downstairs, steadying herself on the banister rail to stop herself from falling. In the kitchen she shoved her shoes back on and found her handbag. She raced for the door, desperate to be out in the cool air. As she slammed the door, she thought she heard Nico shouting after her, but kept going. She cut down an alley out of sight and, by instinct, found her way back to the quay.

Beach Road was half way up a steep hill, but she ploughed on until the lights of her old home came into view. She stood still for a minute and forced herself to take in a series of long, deep yoga breaths until she felt in some semblance of control. The last thing she needed was Annie asking too many questions.

Tish turned her key quietly in the lock and stepped inside.

'I thought you were never coming home. You won't *believe* what I found.' Annie, pale and wide-eyed, stood at the top of the stairs waving one of the small blue books.

A wave of nausea rose in Tish's stomach. What now?

7

So easily Nico could have caught up with her, but he gave up and walked back into the house. What would he say anyway? He couldn't tell her the truth, so it was better for her to think that he was a jerk and a tease. The rigid self-control he'd imposed on himself years ago had shattered when he touched her sweet, soft lips — exactly as he had known it would when she came back into his life.

He needed to speak to the only person who would understand. Nico's fingers shook as he entered Peter's long international number and waited for the connection.

'Hey, little brother, what's up? You're disrupting my beauty sleep.' His brother's deep laugh rumbled down the phone.

'Patricia Treloare's here, she's calling

herself Tish Carlisle these days — and tonight I kissed her.' The words tumbled out over each other. 'Hell, Peter, what am I going to do? I was this close to making love to her.'

'You wouldn't listen to me, would you? I told you to make an excuse and pass her case on to your partner.' Peter's slightly hectoring tone grated on Nico's nerves. 'Dad knew your weakness where she was concerned, why do you think he was so adamant about getting that promise from us both?'

'Would it be so dreadful after all this time?'

He knew the answer, but he needed to ask anyway.

'Don't be naïve. Frank Treloare as good as killed our mother, and the fact she wasn't your birth mother makes no difference. We made the same promise to Dad — never to have anything to do with the Treloare family.' Peter's voice cracked with raw emotion and Nico had no rebuttal. His brother was right.

'It'll take me a few more days to sort

the business out with her house, but once it's done and she's sorted out all her father's possessions, there's nothing to keep her here. Sorry for waking you.'

Peter chuckled. 'Hey, that's OK — you woke Karen too, and I get to take advantage of her now. Good night and hang in there, you're doing the right thing.'

Nico closed up the phone and sat alone, shrouded in darkness. He'd lie here on the sofa and hope he fell asleep — no way could he face being in his bedroom tonight with the searing memory of Tish's sexy body pressed against his. Why was doing the right thing so difficult?

★   ★   ★

Tish took a deep breath and caught hold of the other woman's hands. 'Calm down. Come into the kitchen and we'll make tea. We don't want to wake Jamie, or we'll never get a chance to talk.'

79

Annie glanced anxiously back up the stairs. 'Alright. But I don't know . . . '

'Shush.' Tish led the way and kept busy, filling up the kettle and getting out two mugs and the milk. The situation demanded chocolate, so she found the tin with the dark chocolate almond cookies she'd made the day before. She poured their tea and carried it over to the table, sinking into a chair and kicking off her shoes.

'How was dinner with the elusive Mr De Burgh?' Annie nibbled on a cookie.

'It was OK.' She wasn't about to share any details of her disastrous evening. 'Why do you call him that?'

'Nobody here knows how to take him these days — although any woman with blood running through her veins would like half a chance,' Annie answered with the hint of a smile. 'I'm guessing you remember when he arrived?' Her eyes lit up with barely suppressed curiosity.

'Oh yes.' He was the first boy she'd ever noticed. 'I was eleven and he was thirteen. He came from Sicily to live with the Penwarrens down at the bottom of Cliff Hill. I heard he was a distant cousin, but no one ever said why he'd been sent here and you got the impression you weren't supposed to ask. He was put in the same class as me to start with, because his English wasn't much good and he needed time to catch up.'

Annie cupped the mug in her hands and blew away wisps of steam before taking a sip. 'What was he like?'

'Tall, skinny, and very defensive.' Tish smiled, instantly recalling how prickly and awkward he'd been with everyone. 'But cute. All the girls fell for his soulful eyes and dreamy Italian accent.'

'Did you know the Penwarrens both died?'

Tish's stomach turned. 'No. When?'

'I'm not sure but I think Frank said it was while Nico was at university. He returned here several years later with a different name and the sort of hot Mediterranean looks women swoon over. He must have money from somewhere, judging by the way he dresses and his flashy Alfa Romeo. He's very private, and he and the beautiful Helena appear to have a strange relationship.'

Tish didn't want to talk about Nico any more while she was still upset and confused by their strange encounter. 'Don't worry about him for now. What have you found in Dad's diaries?'

Annie pushed the small worn book across the table. 'This is the one for 1998. Check out the fifteenth of June.'

She opened the book and flipped through until she found the right page.

'You won't like it,' Annie declared bluntly.

'Whatever it says, it's not your fault. I'm the one who suggested reading them after he'd told us not to, so I'm to blame.' Tish concentrated on her father's scratchy writing.

This is wrong. I ought to put a stop to it now. They're practically our neighbours but Elaine's such a sweet woman and she makes me feel I'm a man again instead of a boring nuisance.

'Dad had an affair?' Tish was relieved it wasn't something worse. 'I'm not surprised — my mother always said the reason we left was because he'd been playing around. I really don't need the details.' She closed the book.

'Read the twenty-sixth of July,' Annie said insistently. Tish humoured her and opened the diary back up.

It was very wrong of me to bring her to the house while Eve was out, I don't know what I was thinking — apart from the fact I wasn't. Eve's always had a vicious temper but for once I can't blame her for being furious. I tried to stop her ringing William Penwarren but I couldn't. He came to the door, cursed me for destroying his family and dragged Elaine away. Now

I've destroyed two families because Eve is taking Patricia away tomorrow. They're going to live with her cousin in America. She says I'm not fit to be her father any more . . . and she's right.

'I don't understand.' Tish frowned. 'Mrs Penwarren? This must be a joke. I remember her as a quiet woman who wouldn't say boo to a goose. It can't be her.'

Annie rested her hand on top of Tish's and gave a comforting squeeze. 'I think it must be. People in the village liked and respected your father, which is why I think they've never mentioned this in front of me. Frank only said your mother left with you because the marriage broke down. I didn't ask.'

'They'd argued my whole life and although I freaked out over leaving, in a way it was a relief. I missed Dad terribly for a long time,' Tish muttered in a small, quiet voice.

'How did Nico react when you left?' Annie asked.

'One night I came back from the village youth club and my parents weren't speaking. Mom told me we were leaving in the morning because she couldn't live with Dad any longer. She was so furious I didn't dare ask any questions.

'I tried to sneak downstairs and ring Nico but she caught me and smacked the phone from my hands. She forbade me to write, too, but I disobeyed her when we reached Nashville. He never replied, but I never knew whether he simply didn't write back, or she destroyed them when they arrived.'

'If we've put the story together right, it makes sense that she wouldn't want you to talk to him again. I wonder if he knew? Poor boy,' Annie murmured, her face full of compassion.

'I shouldn't think so. I guess they'd have kept it from him.' She raised her eyes to meet Annie's. 'I don't want to hate Dad.'

'Then don't. He didn't have an easy marriage. If you read some of the earlier diaries you'll see how bad things were.' She hesitated, plainly unsure how much to say. 'I don't think your mother ever really loved him.'

Tish desperately wanted to know her father better — and clearly her mother wouldn't tell her the truth.

'Would you mind if I took the diaries to my room?'

'Help yourself. Should I have kept this to myself?' Annie's sad voice was laden with doubt.

Tish shook her head. 'No. I'd always rather know the truth so I can deal with it face on. I'll see you in the morning.'

* * *

In her bedroom Tish stripped off, tossing her clothes in a heap on the floor. She'd bet anything Nico would hang his up neatly, no matter what. Gently she touched her throat, remembering the way his mouth had burned a

86

trail down her hot skin. He'd wanted her too, despite his denial. They'd messed around as teenagers, but were too scared of the consequences to go very far. Tonight they'd been on the point of having it all before he got scared off.

There could be a million reasons for his frustrating behaviour, from caring for Helena more than he'd admit to just plain oddness. She wasn't about to bring up the subject of Elaine and Frank with him any time soon, even if they got back on speaking terms.

The plan to get in and out of Cornwall as fast as possible was now officially a joke. There were too many loose ends of her father's life for her to leave yet. For the first time in years, her efficient side had smashed into her heart — and stalled.

Tish checked her watch and worked out that it was four in the afternoon in Nashville. Perfect. She could catch Sadie before she left work.

'Tish — finally! I thought you'd

dropped off the face of the planet,' her business partner and best friend yelled. Tish held the phone away from her ear, preferring to have some level of hearing left after their chat.

'Yeah, I know I said I'd be back by now.' Her mind went on autopilot until the other woman slowed down. 'Circumstances have changed and I need to stay longer. If you don't mind chairing the production meeting on Monday I'll love you forever. Get Antony to deal with follow-ups on the overseas orders. Promise him anything he wants and I'll deal with it later.'

Sadie ranted on about how Tish was the face of the business and couldn't wimp out on them this way. She tried not to overreact but it had been a long, tiring day and her emotions were stretched tighter than a drum. *Reminder to self — don't make late night calls when overwrought.*

'Sadie, I'm sorry, but I need to do this. I've some concerns about the new Nashville Icons line but I'll email you the details tomorrow.'

The call ended and Tish sat back on the bed, shocked at the choice she'd made. Would she step further into the unknown tomorrow, or lose her nerve and retreat? She'd never backed down from anything in her adult life and didn't plan to start now.

She reached for her unsexy Mickey Mouse pyjamas and yanked them on, determined to push away the teasing vision of where she might be now had Nico's conscience not got the better of him.

Tish climbed into bed and reached for the next diary, hoping she wouldn't find any more of her father's unwelcome secrets.

8

'Josie, pop these in the afternoon post for me, please.' Nico passed over the two letters he'd spent the last hour putting together.

'Do you have copies for me to file?' She examined the sealed envelopes, giving him a quizzical look.

'No, I've done them.' His blunt reply garnered another stare but he ignored it — and her. He glanced back at his computer, implying he had too much work to be bothered with inane questions. He didn't look back up until she had left the room, slamming his door behind her.

Nico allowed himself a quiet, satisfied smile. By something close to a miracle he'd solved the problem of number six, Beach Road without having to meet Tish again. All he needed now was to stay well away from her until she was thousands of miles away once more.

He'd called in a favour from his old friend, Chris Pope, the local bank manager. Over a fancy lunch washed down with a couple of bottles of the best wine, they'd hashed out an agreement suiting them both. Tish would pay off the mortgage while the bank contacted Annie to say Tish had no desire to live at the house and was willing to rent it to her. They'd set the rent low enough for her to be able to pay it from Frank's small insurance policy. At some point in the future, Tish could raise the subject of signing the house over to Jamie.

This gave her no reason to stay, and he hoped she would take the hint. Nico finished off his stale cup of coffee and got back to work, determined not to think any more about why he felt so damned miserable.

★　★　★

When sketching new ornament designs didn't do the trick, cooking was Tish's go-to therapy. Methodically she chopped onions and peppers and scooped them straight into the hot pan. Thin strips of beef and garlic and ginger went in next as she stirred and tossed the mixture. A dash of soy sauce and rice wine vinegar, and it was ready to taste. Tish's nose wrinkled slightly. A hint of fish sauce and it would be perfect.

'That smells wonderful. I hope it's for lunch, or I'm going to strangle you.' Annie laughed, balancing Jamie on one hip.

'I've puréed some vegetables, too, for this darlin' boy.' Tish grinned at her brother — she'd abandoned the 'half' part because it sounded picky and mean. 'Why don't you feed him while I finish this? The rice is nearly ready.'

'Thanks.' Annie popped Jamie into the white wood high chair and clicked the buckles in place.

'Just so you know, I've read the

diaries up to where you met my Dad. If you prefer me not to read any further, you've got to tell me. I'm not good at guessing what people mean, and in the States we tend to be more straightforward than y'all are.' Tish turned from the stove to face her newly acquired stepmother.

Annie stopped spooning food into Jamie, her face tight and drawn. 'If you don't mind, I'd rather have those back. I'll read them when I'm ready. It's too soon yet.' Her voice thickened with emotion and Tish gave a small nod of agreement.

She wished there was someone to share her conflicting feelings with. The picture her mother had drawn of an uncaring man who'd betrayed his family and shown no interest in his daughter's life was clearly false; his pain at being separated from her shone through every page of his diaries. She'd wasted years hating him, and now regret for failing to return earlier was gnawing at her. She'd come close to telling Nico how she felt because she'd been sure he'd understand — but he'd made it perfectly clear he wanted nothing more to do with her.

'Tish, are you alright? You don't mind too much about the diaries, do you?' Annie's worried voice brought her back.

'No, not at all. I'll dish our lunch up now.' Tish pulled a pretty blue patterned plate towards her. She mounded brown rice in the centre, topped it with a generous portion of the stir-fry and garnished it with a twist of spring onion. 'There you go.'

'Aren't you having any?'

'Of course.' Tish wasn't hungry after last night's set-to with Nico but dished herself up a small portion.

'What are your plans for tonight?' Annie asked.

'Tonight? Nothing special. Why?'

'My friend Janet has free tickets for a play at the Hall for Cornwall in Truro. It's a comedy. Like to come with us?'

'What about Jamie?'

'You didn't think I'd leave him here alone?' Annie grinned and squeezed Tish's hand. 'Don't worry, my mother's coming down from Plymouth this afternoon and staying for a few days.'

'Oh, well, I don't want to be in the way at the play — or while your Mom's here. Would you rather I stayed somewhere else for a couple of days? It won't bother me.' She'd caused enough trouble already by her return, she chided herself.

'Don't be silly. Why do you think she's coming — apart from to dote on Jamie, of course?' Annie snorted.

'I haven't a clue.'

'And here I was thinking you're a smart young woman. Mum can't wait to meet you and size you up,' Annie replied with a twinkling smile.

'Oh, right, I didn't think.' Tish playfully banged her head with her hand. 'Mine would do exactly the same.'

'We'll leave here about five and get a bite to eat before the show. Most people don't dress really fancy to go there, although I will put on a skirt and drag up some make-up from somewhere.' She glanced ruefully down over the worn navy sweat pants she wore most days.

'Sure! It sounds great.' Tish glanced around the untidy kitchen. 'I'll clear up, then I might go out for a walk. I'll take care of Jamie later and give you a chance to get ready.'

'Thanks — your father was right, you're a good girl,' Annie murmured sadly. Tish jumped up and headed over to the sink, staring at the dishes through tear-soaked eyes.

*   *   *

Nico adjusted the knot of his dark green silk tie and checked his appearance in the full-length mirror. Helena didn't ask for much in their undemanding relationship, but she did expect him to be well-dressed when they went out. Normally he enjoyed giving in to his

Italian love of stylish clothes, but tonight he was resentful.

He checked his watch and cursed. He should have left ten minutes ago, and being late was another of Helena's no-no's.

As he ran down the stairs the phone started to ring. Seeing his uncle's number he ignored it, grabbed his keys and headed out of the door. The answering machine could earn its keep. He wasn't in the mood for another of Antonio's lectures tonight.

He strode along the street and up around the corner to his garage. They were a rarity in the centre of Trevayne, but he'd been lucky to find someone willing to rent theirs out for an exorbitant monthly amount. Nico wasn't about to tempt the local bored youths with his new black Alfa Romeo.

He planned to charm Helena into a good mood tonight so that he could wangle an invitation to stay the night with her after the show. Simple, uncomplicated sex, the kind they specialised in, should put a dent in his stirred-up libido.

Nico eased the car out into the street and set off. He kept a reasonable amount over the speed limit all the way there, taking a chance that he wouldn't get stopped unless the local police were in a bad mood. Arriving at her street, he slammed on the brakes and pulled into a space within sight of Helena's flat. For a moment he rested his hands on the steering wheel.

'About time too. Where on earth have you been?' Helena rapped on the window.

Nico unlocked her door and waited for her to get in, receiving an annoyed glare.

'Forgotten our manners tonight, have we?' She slid into the passenger seat and smoothed out a few imaginary creases in her elegant black cocktail dress.

'Sorry. I was running late.' He had a sudden desire to cut his losses and go home, but told himself not to be stupid.

He refused to give a more detailed explanation. There was a lot that Helena didn't or wouldn't understand. Top of the list was why being an ordinary solicitor suited him, and now he mentally added a new one — Tish Carlisle.

'Are you going to drive us to Truro or sit here all night?'

Nico snapped out of his musing and drove all the way to Truro without saying another word. They had a brief discussion about where to park and found a spot close by in Lemon Street. Avoiding a repeat of his earlier mistake he jumped quickly out of the car, then ran around to open her door. Helena got out and Nico risked dropping a quick kiss on her smooth cheek.

'You look lovely.' The sleeveless black dress showed off her tall, slender figure, and tonight her sleek blonde hair was drawn back in a neat French pleat. Nothing about her was showy or ostentatious and her make-up was always discreet, along with her light floral perfume. She was the kind of woman other men looked at with envy when they were out together.

She slipped her arm through his. 'How's your week been?'

That was her way of accepting his apology. A normal girlfriend would genuinely want to know, but he understood the rules well enough to give the expected answer. She'd be mortified if he told her about Tish and the tangle he'd got himself into.

'Fine, how was yours?'

'My case should wrap up next week.'

'Do you expect to win?' he asked and Helena threw him a confused look.

'Of course. What a strange thing to say.'

Nico thought it was pretty normal, but she didn't see it that way and the conversation died as they arrived at the hall. He pulled out the tickets and ushered her into the foyer.

'Mr De Burgh? Well! Fancy seeing you here.'

Swivelling around, he met Annie Treloare's bright, curious eyes. Before he could get his mind together and answer he glanced over her shoulder and froze. Tish's bright, teasing smile filled his gaze, rendering him speechless. She stepped forward to join them, her hips swaying gently inside a full-skirted red and white polka dot dress. Nico itched to wrap his hands around her narrow waist, cinched in with a wide, white belt, and pull her up against him before he . . .

'Nico, aren't you going to introduce me to your friends?' Helena's sharp voice startled him back to awareness.

Tish stuck out her hand, the action tightening the strapless dress around her generous breasts and threatening Nico's wafer-thin hold on sanity. 'I'm Tish Carlisle. Nico and I are old friends. I'm sure he's told you all about me.' The mischievous tilt of her glossy red lips set his senses reeling.

'I don't believe he has.' Helena's icy tone boded ill for later. Forget happy, uncomplicated sex. He'd be in for an interrogation.

'It's a pleasure to meet you. We'd better find our seats but perhaps we'll see you at the interval.'

'Sure thing. Let's meet at the bar and have a good chat.'

Nico met Tish's sparkling eyes head-on and wanted to smack her for being so childish.

'It'll be our pleasure, won't it, Nico?' Helena skewered him with a false smile.

All he could do was agree and hope that the ceiling fell in on the building before the end of Act One.

9

'He's got his hands full there.' Tish's hands rested on her hips and she tapped one bright red stiletto on the tiled floor.

'She's very beautiful,' Annie ventured.

'If you want to snuggle up with an iceberg,' Tish mocked.

'Who was the hunk?' Janet Truscott asked, bubbling over with curiosity. 'I haven't seen anything as tasty for a long time.'

'Nico De Burgh,' Annie answered. 'He's Sicilian, which is why he's so hot. I always think he should be on the cover of a men's fashion magazine. A woman could sink into those deep brown eyes and stay there a very long time.' She grinned. 'He was Frank's solicitor, so this lucky girl's been dealing with him about the house.'

Thin frown lines creased her forehead, and Tish wished she could reassure her.

'What a hardship. I thought he was going to eat you up, Tish,' Janet teased.

Embarrassment flamed in her face. 'Whatever do you mean?' She tried to sound puzzled.

'Oh, come on, it's obvious he's got the hots for you.' Janet poked her arm.

'He came close to drooling.' Annie joined in with the fun.

'We had a brief romance years ago. End of story.' If this pair found out about the sizzling kiss, and more, they'd shared the other night they'd be remorseless.

'If you say so.' Annie exchanged a knowing look with her friend. 'Let's go and find our seats.'

★   ★   ★

'We have five minutes, Nico, before the play starts. I suggest you give me a quick rundown on your friend,' Helena

104

ordered in the tone which put fear into every criminal she prosecuted, and more than a few judges and fellow lawyers.

Nico fiddled with the programme, pretending to check out the cast list. 'We became friends after I moved here and dated a bit as teenagers. That's it, really.' *Liar. You loved her then and you're a hair's width away from loving her again.* 'I was her father's solicitor and he died recently, so she's returned from the States to sort out his estate.' He purposely kept it vague.

'Don't be naïve. You're stupid if you can't see she's trying to get her claws into you. I didn't appreciate the way you stared back at her, either. Goodness knows where she found that old dress — I'm guessing the nearest charity shop.' Helena snorted.

Nico couldn't defend Tish without dropping himself in even more trouble. He bit his lip. 'You're exaggerating her interest, and I certainly haven't encouraged her.' He deserved a Pinocchio nose for spouting such a blatant lie.

'I should certainly hope not,' Helena snapped.

'Leave it, Helena.' He turned away to face the stage as the orchestra struck up the introductory music. An old-fashioned farce with double entendre jokes wouldn't suit his strange mood but at least it would stop Helena talking for a while, and should be an improvement on the depressing Ibsen play she'd dragged him along to last month.

The interval arrived far too quickly and he made one more attempt to escape from what was bound to be a disaster. 'We don't have to go to the bar. Let's stay here.'

Helena's disbelieving glare pinned him to the seat.

'Don't be ridiculous. Where are your manners tonight, Nico? Of course we're going.' She stood up and tucked her velvet clutch bag into the crook of her arm. 'Let's get it over with.'

Nico left Helena at a table and made

his way steadily through the chattering crowd, relieved not to spot Tish or her cohorts. He reached the bar unaccosted and leaned on the counter.

'Lookin' for someone, handsome?' The combination of Tish's soft drawl right by his ear and her warm, musky scent sent a rush of blood straight to his groin.

'What the devil are you playing at?' he hissed and her eyes widened in fake innocence.

'Why, Mr De Burgh, whatever do you mean?'

'Do you normally make eyes at a man when he's out with his girlfriend for the night?'

Her bubbling laughter rippled through him — no doubt she thought him the most pompous man on the planet, but it was sheer self-preservation on his part.

'I'm just being friendly. Must be the Southern habits I've picked up. Obviously you still prefer the whole uptight, reserved English thing.' She stroked one long red fingernail along his arm, sending a jolt of electricity through his suit jacket and searing his skin. 'You'd be much more fun if you relaxed a little.'

'May I offer you and your friends a drink?' he asked as politely as he could manage through gritted teeth.

She smirked right back at him. 'I'll let you change the subject for now, but we're not through.'

Oh yes we are. 'Drinks.'

'One Chardonnay, one orange and lemonade and . . . ' She licked her glossy scarlet lips and he ached to seize her mouth and kiss it all off. 'You can get me a gin and tonic.'

'Right. I'll bring the drinks over. Where are you sitting?'

She pointed, and leaned closer to brush her lips against his cheek. 'Thanks, Nico,' she whispered. With a wicked smile she left him, painfully aroused and nowhere near a cold shower. Nothing seemed to dampen his fierce desire for the woman he'd sworn never to touch again.

'Ok there, ladies?' Tish beamed at the three women. 'Our saviour is fighting the crowd, bringing enough drinks to get us through the second act of this drivel.'

'I assume you're not a fan of Restoration farce, Miss Carlisle?' Helena asked in a snide tone.

'If you mean men in wigs and tights running around after women falling out of their dresses, I'll go with a no.' She eyed her rival. 'I can't imagine it's your scene either, sweetheart.'

'If you understand the deeper meanings in the humour, it's possible to gain insights into the human condition.' Helena smoothed a single, rogue hair back into place.

Tish suppressed the urge to wipe the supercilious smile right off her snooty face.

'There we go. I hope I got the orders right.' Nico placed a loaded tray down on the small round table.

Tish seized her drink and knocked half of it back in one swallow, savouring the warm kick in the base of her stomach. She strained to catch what Annie was saying to Nico.

'I know I shouldn't mention business here but I need to come and see you next week.' She flushed slightly, suddenly aware of Tish's interest. 'I must know where I stand.'

He patted her hand with surprising kindness. 'I promise, by next week we'll sort it all out. Please try not to worry.'

'But — ' Tish tried to interrupt but Nico's stern glare stopped her dead in her tracks. He was right, they had an agreement and he was a professional where the law was concerned. She sat back in the chair as he deftly steered the conversation back to safer subjects such as the unpredictable weather and Jamie's progress. Annie chatted happily about her son as Janet joined in, adding her praises of the bright little boy.

Tish sipped on her gin and wished it contained less tonic water. She checked out Helena while the other woman wasn't aware — her beautiful face marred by utter disinterest. Whatever was the hot-blooded Nico doing with such a cold woman?

Remembering his anger at the lack of self-control he'd shown around her, it dawned on her. With Helena he'd never be tempted to let go completely, and for some reason he needed that level of discipline in his life.

A surge of pity swept through Tish at realising what a lonely man he'd grown up to be. At that moment Nico met her gaze and for a few magical seconds the world stopped, along with her own breath.

The five-minute bell rang and it was time to return to their seats. Tish remained glued to the chair as Nico deliberately turned away, stood up and held out his hand to Helena.

'It was a pleasure to meet you all. Enjoy the rest of the play.' Helena's polite, dutiful comments drifted over Tish's head and all she did was nod and watch them leave.

Something tugged at her hand and she gave a start, suddenly aware of the warm room and the shifting crowd.

'Are you going to sit there all night?' Annie asked.

'Sorry. Let's go.' She followed Janet out of the bar. The spark had gone from the evening; Nico had taken it with him.

10

'That's strange.' Annie frowned, checking through the morning post. 'We've both got a letter from the delectable Mr De Burgh.' She passed one to Tish and started to open her own.

Tish took another sip of tea and played with the envelope.

'Oh, my goodness.' Annie's hand flew up to cover her mouth. 'This is wonderful.' She turned and half-glared, half-grinned at Tish. 'Why didn't you tell me? You're close-mouthed, I must say. Even when my dear mother was prying, you never said a word. This is wonderful. Thank you so much.'

Trying to keep her expression neutral Tish slipped a fingernail under the seal and pulled out the single sheet of paper.

'Well, say something,' Annie persisted.

'Hang on a minute. Let me read

through what he's got to say.' She'd ignored Nico's calls and texts all day yesterday, sure he'd harp on about Saturday night. It hadn't occurred to her that he wanted to talk about the house. Scanning through his brief explanation, she couldn't believe he'd pulled it off.

'I told Nico I didn't need the house, but there were a few financial problems. Happily he solved it with the bank.'

Annie threw her arms around Tish's neck, pulling her into a smothering hug. 'It's more than great. I'd have had no choice but to move home with my mum and dad. Who wants to do that at forty?' She bubbled with excitement and Tish's throat tightened on a sob. Nico's behaviour was irrelevant, compared to the fact that her little brother would have a settled home.

'I'm happy it's worked out, too. Why don't you go and see to Jamie while I fix breakfast? I'll probably pop into Truro later for a little shopping.'

She was only bending the truth a

little. She would check out a vintage clothing shop someone had mentioned, but only after she turned up in his office to thank Nico whether he liked it or not. To hell with their 'agreement'.

* * *

Tish stepped out of the car and took a deep breath of the warm summer air. Making sure she'd locked up, she headed towards the centre of town. Near the cathedral, she took off down a side street and stopped half way down outside the door of Nico's office. For a minute she held back.

At sixteen she'd been dragged away from everything familiar and thrown into a high school where being the stuck-up English kid made her the bullies' number one target. She overcame it all, excelled in college and was hugely successful in a business she loved. Why an emotionally stunted, bad-tempered, no-account solicitor in a small Cornish town bothered her so much was beyond annoying.

Before she could think too much more, Tish pushed open the door and stepped inside.

* * *

Nico's hands pressed down into the desk and he didn't dare turn around. The subtle hint of warm spice announced Tish's arrival as surely as any trumpet fanfare, but he pretended to finish sorting out a few mistakes in a letter with Josie.

'Thanks. I'll be in my office if anything's unclear.'

Only barely glancing over his shoulder, he finally spoke to her.

'Please follow me, Miss Carlisle.'

He made it all the way in and settled in his chair before he actually looked at her.

Hell. How could she make a simple white shirt knotted at the waist and skinny black jeans so damn sexy? Nico clasped his hands together and prepared to finish this once and for all before he cracked and grabbed hold of her again.

'I assume you received my letter this morning?'

She nodded, but he continued before she could interrupt the speech he'd planned out. 'I did try to contact you before finalising things but ... ' He shrugged, careful not to say she hadn't answered or returned any of his calls. 'I believe the arrangement should be to everyone's satisfaction. Do you have any questions?'

Tish plopped down into the chair and stretched out. 'Have you quite finished being pompous?'

Tension rippled through his shoulder blades and settled in the back of his neck. 'Do you have any questions, Tish?'

A teasing smile pulled at her glossy scarlet lips. 'Fine. Have it your way. It all seems straightforward enough. I suppose you've got forms for me to sign?'

'They're all ready.' Nico opened the

manila folder in front of him and removed four papers, pushing them across the table towards her. 'I've marked all the places to be initialled and at the end of the document you sign in full. If you wish to confer with the bank manager I can make those arrangements.'

Tish shook her head. 'It won't be necessary.'

Nico studied her under the guise of checking some other documents. She read through everything carefully, unlike a lot of his clients who signed anything he put in front of them. He found it hard to get his head around the fact that the dreamy teenage girl he'd known was now a successful businesswoman.

'Yes, I can read. Amazing, isn't it?' The teasing glance she tossed in his direction further tightened his nerves into knots.

'Don't imply you know what I'm thinking.'

Tish stilled and the humour died in

her eyes. 'I'm sorry. Believe it or not, I really appreciate what you've done here.' She lowered her gaze to the papers under her fingers. 'I wish you could've seen Annie's face when she read the letter. I hadn't realised how worried she was until she wasn't any more — if that makes sense?' She glanced back up and drew him in to a place with no way of escape.

He couldn't hold back on touching her a second longer and slid his hands on top of hers, cupping the long fingers and massaging her warm, trembling skin. 'You've done the right thing. Your father would be proud of you.'

'Do you really think so?' The shimmer of tears filling her pretty eyes slammed in to Nico.

'Yes, in so many ways.' He wished he could ask the same question about his own father.

'Thanks,' she whispered in her soft, breathy voice.

Nico startled at a loud knock on his door and jerked his hands back to his lap as his secretary walked into the room.

Josie gave him a strange look. 'There's a Mrs Annie Treloare on the line. Do you want to speak to her?'

He cleared his throat and struggled to get his brain back in some sort of working order. 'Certainly. Put her through.'

Tish made a move to leave but he gestured at her to sit still and picked up the phone. For several minutes he couldn't get a word in edgeways as Annie thanked him over and over again. Nico caught Tish's smile and without thinking gave in and smiled back. He heard a disembodied voice and realised poor Annie was asking if he was still there.

'Yes, of course I am. I didn't want to interrupt you. I need you to come into my office when it's convenient and sign some papers. Apart from that, you're all set.' He didn't look at Tish.

'My pleasure,' he responded with a smile and hung up.

'Can I thank you too, or have you had enough of women fawning over you?'

'A man never gets tired of being thought clever.' He grinned and leaned back in the chair, resting his hands behind his head.

'I suppose you only did it so quickly to get me out of your hair. You must be happy there's nothing to keep me here now?'

He refused to rise to her taunt. 'You've work to get back to?'

Tish frowned. 'Yes, plenty, but I think my staff can hold it together for a week or so. This weather's a lot better than the ninety-degree humidity I left Nashville suffering.'

He ought to say something, anything, but he was as tongue-tied as he'd been at fifteen and longing to kiss her for the first time. Tish stood up and slung her silver bag over her shoulder.

'I'd better be off. Maybe I'll see you around before I leave?'

He got up and walked around the desk to join her. 'Perhaps. I'd appreciate it if you let my secretary know the date of your departure in case there are any loose ends to tie up.'

She winced at his cold manner but Nico couldn't apologise.

'I will.' Tish thrust out her hand, forcing him to touch her again. He clasped it with his own and the brush of her heated skin sent shivers racing through his overheated body. 'Take care.'

'You too,' he murmured, staring down at his shoes, completely unable to look at her any more.

She pulled her hand loose and ran from his office, the sound of her shoes clattering on the wood stairs as she raced from the building. Nico gripped the edge of the desk, afraid his legs would buckle if he tried to move. He stayed there a long time because the only alternative was to follow her.

★ ★ ★

Tish didn't stop running until she reached her car. Her hand shook as she tried to fit the key in the lock but somehow she jerked open the door and fell into the seat. *Damn, Nico.* She hoped he suffered too, because he deserved it. What would he have said if she'd challenged him about their parents' supposed affair? Tish couldn't envision putting it into words. If she ever did, Nico's coolness would turn to ice and they'd surely never speak again.

Five days. She'd finish sorting through her father's things and spend time with Annie and Jamie before she got back to work. The Las Vegas trade show was scheduled for the first week in August, and a must on her calendar. Sadie had their display all planned and it would be their big push for next year's orders. Tish started up the car and put it smoothly into gear for the first time, unable to resist a satisfied smile. She couldn't face doing any shopping today. The last couple of nights, when she wasn't dreaming of

Nico, she'd begun to see images of Cornish-inspired designs which would make unique ornaments. She'd get some down on paper; it would be a far more constructive use of her time than hanging around in case a certain man unbent enough to make a move on her.

11

Nico's willpower ebbed away as the level sank in the grappa bottle. He should be pleased that everything had gone as planned today, but instead he was hollow inside.

He'd come close to phoning Tish multiple times since she fled from his office. Hours ago he moved the phone from his pocket to the table and it had stared accusingly back at him ever since. Teasing. Just like damn Tish Carlisle. He pressed number one on his speed dial.

'Hey, baby, what're you doing tonight?' He enunciated the words carefully.

'Nico? You're drunk.' Helena's razor-sharp voice cut through his mental fog. If he wanted sympathy, his so-called girlfriend was the wrong person to ask.

'I might've had a few drinks but I'm fine. How about you come over and see me?' He needed her, but wasn't stupid enough to spell it out and be laughed at. They didn't do 'need'.

'I've got to finish putting this new case together by tomorrow. I don't have time for your drunken ramblings. I suggest you drink a glass of water, take a couple of aspirin and go to bed.'

Bed. Exactly what he had in mind — but he was pretty sure she didn't fancy the idea, or him, tonight.

'Please, sweetheart.' Nico sighed. Another rule broken, but he needed saving from himself.

'Good night. I'll see you on Wednesday as usual, if you're sober by then.' She hung up.

Nico tossed the phone onto the table and slumped back against the sofa cushions. He picked up the remote control and turned on the football.

* * *

Tish curled her legs up under her on the sofa and took out her sketchpad.

Images swirled in her head and with swift strokes of her charcoal pencil, the first attempt emerged. This was her favourite part of the process. Before long she had lost herself in her work, and within an hour she had the bare bones of a new line of ornaments.

Traditional Celtic designs were too obvious and already available, so she was thinking more on the lines of Cornish-inspired decorations connected to the sea, the coastline and the moors. She needed to do more research, but being here again had re-energised her creative side.

Her stomach growled and Tish remembered she'd turned down Annie's offer of sausages and baked beans earlier. Jamie hadn't slept well last night and stayed up all day, which meant he and his mother were worn out and in bed already.

She craved company. It was beyond stupid, but she picked up her phone and entered the numbers she'd memorised before she could change her mind.

She guessed he must be out.

'Changed your mind? I thought you would.' Nico's low rumbling laugh echoed in her ear.

'Whatever are you talking about?'

'Who is this?'

Very flattering. How many other American women did he talk to on a regular basis? 'It's Tish.'

'Oh, hell.'

'Charming. I'm so glad I called.' *Stupid, stupid mistake.*

'Hey, don't hang up. I was . . . sleeping.'

'Bit early, isn't it?' Tish softened a little, imagining him stretched out on his sofa, his feet hanging over the edge.

'The football wasn't very interesting.'

'Obviously not.' She resolved to spell it out and wait to be rejected again. 'I've been working all day and I'm starving. I suppose you've eaten?'

'Uh, no.'

He was *really* slow tonight. Either that or he was too polite to tell her to get lost — again.

'Nico, if you won't ask I'll be brazen. Would you care to have dinner with me?'

A lengthy silence. She was on the verge of hanging up.

'I . . . I suppose it'd be OK,' he muttered.

'Don't be too enthusiastic.'

'Oh, Tish, you caught me unawares, that's all. I can't pick you up because I've had a couple of beers but I could meet you at the Blue Anchor?'

Not quite what she had in mind, but she'd take what she could get tonight. 'Fine. I'll see you there in an hour.'

Her stomach might be hollow, but no way was she having another shot at Nico without changing out of the jeans she'd been wearing all day. The perfect dress for tonight hung in the wardrobe, an original 1920s flapper dress she'd picked up in Paris last year. Made of pale pink silk and worn with a single long knotted strand of pearls and pink low-heeled shoes, it was far too stylish for the Blue Anchor ... but not for Mr De Burgh.

Maybe today wouldn't be a dead loss after all.

★   ★   ★

Nico allowed the icy shards of water to slice into him for a full five minutes. A vigorous rub with a warm towel got the circulation going again and he headed back into the bedroom. He selected a white linen shirt and tan trousers, laying them neatly on the bed. At the base of his skull the beginnings of a hangover pulled at his senses, making him too weary to think too deeply about why she'd rung.

He concentrated on getting dressed, then stood in front of the mirror and combed his thick brown hair, noticing it could do with a trim. Running his fingers over his jaw, he considered shaving but rejected the idea on the grounds that he wasn't out to impress

Tish . . . plus his hands weren't quite steady.

Keys, phone and wallet went in his pockets and he checked the time. Knowing Tish, she'd be late.

Nico strolled down the street, greeting a couple of neighbours. He supposed they'd call him an honorary local after all these years, but he still only had acquaintances rather than friends. He didn't get close to people any more because it opened a person up to loss and pain, and he'd had enough of both for a lifetime.

'There you are!' Tish's brash, throaty laugh startled him as he walked around the corner. 'Beat you to it for once.' She couldn't have looked happier if she'd won the lottery jackpot.

'I'd chalk it up to luck if I were you,' he commented, hearing his cynical, steady voice and totally amazed at how opposed it was to his feelings, the overwhelming desire flooding his body.

Nico was sober enough to realise he was half-drunk; not a good condition in which to make decisions. The sight of Tish, a vision in pale pink, made the breath tighten in his throat. The thin silk skimmed over her delicious curves as if she wore nothing but bare skin. As he took one step closer, her warm spicy scent aroused his senses and against his will Nico reached out and stroked the curve of her shoulder.

'Beautiful,' he growled and bent to press his lips against the throbbing pulse in her neck. Nico slid his hands down to wrap around her waist, but she pushed him away, hard, making him almost fall down on the cobblestones.

'What was that for?' He regained his balance and glared.

'You're drunk.' Anger mixed with a touch of amusement in her voice. 'Get inside and we'll eat.' She moved towards the door and threw him a saucy glance back over her shoulder. 'And keep your hands to yourself unless I tell you otherwise.'

Who did she think she was? 'I'm not hungry,' he growled.

'Don't be childish. You need something to soak up all the — ' Tish rose up on her tiptoes level with his mouth and sniffed — 'vodka you've poured down.'

'Grappa. No self respecting Sicilian drinks vodka.' He smirked and she slipped her arm into the crook of his elbow.

'Come on. I'm starving.'

Nico allowed her to lead the way, his brain telling him he should have stayed at home. He'd never shown any sense around this woman before, so why would he start now?

12

'This haddock is great — I sure do miss good English fish and chips.' Tish put another forkful in her mouth and relished the contrast between the crunchy batter and sweet, flaky fish.

'Hard to beat, isn't it? I'm not much for fancy food.' He shoved a large piece of sausage onto his fork and dipped it in the puddle of ketchup on the plate.

She hesitated, wanting to ask Nico something which might put his back up again.

'Go on — you've never been shy before.' He scooped up a forkful of mashed potatoes smothered in thick onion gravy.

Tish was disconcerted about being read so clearly but ploughed on. 'Do you miss genuine Sicilian food? I know there are plenty of Italian restaurants around, but they don't compare to the real thing. I was at a trade show in Florence last year and ate the best food ever.'

His fingers clenched around the fork so hard she thought he might perform a Uri Geller act on the metal.

'It's been a long time.' The terse words hung between them, but she'd gone this far so there was no point holding back now.

'You were thirteen. That's a lot of memories.'

'Arancini, pasta al nivuro di Siccia and my mother used to make the most amazing Cassata . . . ' Nico's gruff voice trailed away to nothing and his usually warm brown eyes filled with dark, unrelenting pain. Tish slid her hand across the table and rested it on top of his, giving a gentle squeeze.

'I'm sorry.' A flush travelled up her neck.

Nico cleared his throat. 'I don't . . . I can't talk about them.'

'Even now?' she murmured.

'Even now. We all have ways of

coping, Tish, this is mine.' The sad finality of his words tore at her heart.

'So, when are you leaving?'

She startled at his blunt question.

'Um, next Friday probably. I haven't booked a ticket yet.'

'Would you like a pudding?' Nico's well-mannered, polite façade slid back into place.

'No, thanks, it's late. I'd better head back.'

'Would you care for a coffee at my place first?'

Tish scrutinised his expressionless face, trying to work out what was behind the seemingly casual question.

'Are you sure? Be honest. You don't have to offer for the sake of being polite. We're long past that, Nico.'

'Of course — and I'll walk you back afterwards.'

'Alright. I'll take you at face value and accept.' Tish gathered up her bag and stood, tossing a sliver of pale pink silk around her shoulders. 'You coming?'

Nico's hard stare sent a shiver right down to her toes and for a second she froze.

'Why not?'

There were plenty of reasons, but she wasn't about to mention them now. Her body craved his touch and she was pretty sure his control balanced on a knife-edge.

They made their way through the crowd of late evening drinkers and stepped outside the pub. 'I'll walk slower this time. I suppose you're wearing more ankle-twisters?' He slid his gaze down over her bare legs and burst into loud, unrestrained laughter. 'Low heels. You came prepared, didn't you?'

'Maybe.' Her stomach flipped pleasantly at the searing glance he threw right back, and she reached up to drag a finger down his cheek. She allowed it to linger when she reached the dark stubble covering his jaw. The roughness excited her and all she could think of was how wonderful it would feel rubbed all over her soft skin.

Nico's arm slid down to circle her waist, and this time she didn't push him away. Perhaps he was still a little drunk, but she didn't care. She'd satisfy her curiosity tonight.

He lowered his mouth to hers and she gasped at the possessive press of his warm, firm lips. She opened to his exploring tongue, revelling in his taste, spicy with a hint of grappa. His large, sure hands cupped her rear and he rocked his hardening arousal against her. Gasping, Tish wriggled closer, desperate for so much more.

'I need to make love with you, Tish. It's been somewhere in my mind for the last fourteen years.'

'Snap. Let's go, or we'll shock the locals.' Tish glanced around, but saw only a couple of curious seagulls.

They dragged each other away from the harbour and up the maze of narrow streets to Nico's house. He shoved the key in the lock, kicked open the door and pulled her inside before slamming the door behind them.

He thrust her up hard against the wall and seized her mouth in another devastating kiss, both of them open-mouthed and desperate. Nico shoved her dress up out of the way, exposing the pink satin thong she'd worn — just in case.

'Oh, God. You're going to kill me.' His long finger slid under the thin string and pressed into her melting core, testing and teasing. 'Upstairs. I need a bed for what I intend to do with you.'

Roughly Nico yanked her dress back down and seized her hand. They stumbled up the stairs together and into his bedroom where he immediately ripped back the duvet and tossed it to the floor. 'Come here.' He peeled the dress up over her head and threw it carelessly on the bedside chair.

Suddenly he went eerily still. Tish trembled as he reached out and stroked over her flimsy pink satin bra, his fingers making slow, lazy circles on her aching breasts. With a swift move he unclasped the bra and allowed it to fall to the floor.

'So lovely.' His low, raspy voice turned her on beyond all rational sense.

'Touch me, please,' she begged.

'Here?' He cupped her with both hands and squeezed. 'I bet you're sweet there too.' Nico's mouth lowered and he began to lick and suck, moaning deep in the back of his throat. 'Honey.'

Tish slipped her hand between them and caressed him through his trousers. 'You're not playing fair. It's my turn.'

He gave a borderline sweet smile, the sort she remembered receiving when her sixteen-year-old self wanted to touch him but was too scared.

'Go on. You know I won't force you, but I won't say no either.'

The zip wouldn't move far and she flashed a quick grin. 'You'll have to help or it could be painful.'

He cupped her hand and between them they eased him open. Tish took over and pushed aside his boxers, freeing him to her exploration. Nico hissed in a deep desperate breath as she wrapped her fingers around his silken length. She stroked up and down, loving the sense of power as he twitched and expanded further in her fingers.

'It'll be over in a matter of seconds if you keep going, cara, my love. I'm aching to be inside you. You have to know that, Tish,' he groaned.

'Come on, get undressed. I'll admire you more later.'

He touched her chin, lifting her face to meet his intense gaze.

'Do you promise?' he murmured huskily.

'Oh yeah, no question.'

His clothes were gone in seconds and Nico swept her up into his arms. Two large strides and he placed her on the bed, kneeling in front of her and devouring her with his eyes.

'Every day since you walked back in my life I've imagined you here.' His smile made her heart clench. He knelt between her legs and trailed his fingers from the throbbing pulse in her neck to another, more intimate place.

'Next time you'll have subtlety and romance — but not tonight.' Nico leaned over and reached into his bedside drawer, tossing several foil packets onto the bed. Efficiently he readied himself for her and shifted back over.

'No more talk,' she pleaded.

A broad, sexy grin spread across his face. 'I love a decisive woman.' He centered himself and with a single unerring thrust filled her body. Tish's hips undulated, urging him on and he adjusted to her rhythm, pounding into her until she was on the point of exploding. His hand slid between them and caressed her, sending Tish screaming over the edge. Their eyes met and she saw pure lust and something indefinable before he plunged one last time, roaring into his own release.

Their burning bodies meshed together as gradually their racing heartbeats returned to normal. Tish cried out as he slid from her and rolled onto his side.

'Don't,' she whispered into his skin.

'I'll crush you.' He gathered a handful of her hair, lifting it to his lips. 'You always smell so good.'

Tish shivered at his sexy, heavily accented drawl.

'You're cold. I'll get the covers.' Nico leapt from the bed and shook out the duvet, throwing it on top of her before climbing back in.

With his arms wrapped tightly around her, Tish's only coherent thought was that this was what she'd been searching for, without even realising it. The timing was wrong to share her revelation with him, and for now she'd simply savour finally being able to say Nico was hers. The fact he wasn't aware of it yet was irrelevant. She could be patient.

13

Clutching her shoes in one hand, Tish inched open the front door. As she stepped out into the street, she exhaled the breath she'd been holding.

'Going somewhere, cara?' Nico's deep, rumbling voice startled her and she jerked around.

'Do you normally leave your lovers this way?' His accent thickened, the way it always did when he was emotional.

Tish stepped back inside with a sigh. 'I don't think we want to give your neighbours a show. You were sleeping like the dead and I wanted to get on back to the house. I'd prefer Annie didn't think I was a — '

'Tart? Slut?' He glowered, his eyes black in the early morning light. 'We're both well over the age of consent, it's nobody else's business.' Nico took a step closer and his hot, angry breath seared her skin. 'Are you ashamed already? It didn't take long.' He loomed over her as she backed up against the door.

Tish took a chance and reached up to rest her hand against his cheek. 'Oh, Nico, don't turn all brooding on me. You're reading too much into this.'

'Are you talking about the fact you're sneaking out, or for sleeping with me in the first place?'

'You're such a typical lawyer sometimes. Don't pick apart every word I say.' She slid her arms around his neck and began to massage the rigid muscles under her fingers.

'I'm sorry — I woke and reached for you and the bed was empty. I'm not good at . . . this.' He stroked her loose hair.

'Me neither.'

Nico rubbed his thumb down to the curve of her neck and she arched into his unnerving touch.

'I've got some thinking to do about Helena. We promised to be faithful and

I'm disappointed in myself.'

The slight twist of a smile pulled at his mouth and he teased her lips with his searching tongue. 'You're intoxicating, Tish.'

For her heart's sake she should back away now, but instead she pressed up longingly against his rock-hard arousal, barely constrained by the thin fabric of his black pyjama trousers.

'She deserves better than the way I've behaved.' His penetrating eyes rested on Tish and she pushed him away.

'So do I.'

Nico took a step back. 'You're right. I apologise. I don't know what I was thinking.' He shoved his fingers through his uncombed hair, but one unruly strand still fell across his brow and she itched to push it away.

'I won't say I had too much to drink or that you're the sexiest woman I've ever met. Those are pathetic excuses for my lack of self control.'

'Thanks — you certainly know the right things to say to a woman who's spent the night in your bed.' She didn't attempt to hide her disgust with his feeble remarks.

'Oh Tish, I'm not sorry we made love because I've always wanted you, but I am sorry for the circumstances. I'll have to be honest and tell Helena. Whether she'll forgive me is out of my hands.' He shrugged.

'Do you want her to?'

'She's a good woman,' he stated, his face blank.

Tish scoffed. 'Oh, come off it, Nico. You don't love her. I've seen you together and there's more passion in a bag of chips.'

Anger suffused his dark features and she knew she'd gone too far. 'Sorry. I shouldn't have said that,' she muttered.

'It's OK. Don't worry about it.'

Tish's chin instantly shot up. 'I don't intend to. You're the one with a girlfriend. I'm a free agent and I believe I'll stay that way too. At least now I've satisfied my curiosity.'

'What do you mean?' He frowned.

'Ever since we fooled around as teenagers I've wanted to have sex with you.' She'd be as unromantic as possible to quash any notion of caring. She dragged her gaze down over him and gave a sly smile as his arousal grew more prominent under her penetrating stare.

'Were you disappointed?' Nico's sarcastic tone and cold glare cut through her and Tish shook her head, unable to lie.

'Not at all. I'd say you're pretty good.' She kept her voice casual and unaffected, while all she really wanted was for him to show her how damn good he was . . . all over again.

'You aren't unique, though. I can get good sex elsewhere and next time it'll be with someone who doesn't beat himself up with guilt afterwards.' She bent down and slipped on her shoes. 'Goodbye, Nico. I'm sure the rest my father's business can be sorted out by mail. Seeing you again isn't on my agenda.'

He remained silent as she struggled with the door, his features etched in stone. Tish's shaking hands finally got it open and she stalked back out into the street . . . out of his life, again.

The cold early morning drizzle penetrated her thin silky dress and Tish shivered as she ran along the street, down to the harbour. She should go straight up the hill, but something about the cold, grey sea pulled her closer. Leaning over the old stone wall she stared at the horizon as tears trickled down her face, mixing with the soft rain. For the first time in years big, heaving sobs shook her body. For her father. For what could have been with Nico. For the life she'd made which now seemed so empty.

This wasn't like her. She'd stopped being sorry for herself a long time ago. Plenty of children survived divorce, moving to another country, a mother who tried but never quite got it right with men, and an apparently disinterested father.

Tish straightened up and tugged at her dress, trying to pull it away from her wet skin. She plastered on a big, fake smile.

Tish Carlisle. Stop this right now. Run back to the house and jump into a hot shower. Afterwards get dressed and fix yourself a big breakfast. You're better than this, so go and prove it again.

She hurried off into the misty grey haze, ready to take on the world again. Nico De Burgh could go to hell.

14

For a woman who'd been made love to all night then ripped apart in the morning, Tish considered that she looked remarkably normal. She fastened the top button of her white Peter Pan blouse to hide the vivid marks Nico's teeth had left on her tender skin. The one he'd left on her heart would take far longer to fade. She fumbled around the top of the dresser but could find only one of the silver earrings she'd worn last night. It would have to stay at Nico's — she wasn't going back there any time soon.

'You look nice.' Annie stood in the bedroom door balancing a gurgling Jamie on her hip. He flailed his arms towards Tish for her to take him. 'Not now, Jamie boy. Tish doesn't want to go out covered in baby slobber.' Absently she wiped at a damp patch he'd drooled on her shoulder.

'Sorry, sweetie — I'll make up for it tonight. Annie, if you'd like to go out, Jamie and I will have some spoiling time together.' She left unspoken the words — *before I leave.* There was only so long she could impose on her stepmother's hospitality.

Annie beamed. 'That'd be great, actually. Janet was wanting to go out for a drink sometime this week but I said I couldn't.'

'Call her back right now and say yes.' Tish laughed, feeling good inside for the first time in hours.

'I will.' Annie glanced back over her shoulder. 'You aren't meeting the gorgeous, brooding Nico again tonight, then?'

Tish stiffened. She wasn't ready to talk about him and what a screw-up she'd made of things.

'No.' The short blunt answer struck home and Annie's face filled with pity.

'Things didn't go well last night, then?'

Tears pricked the back of Tish's eyes but she forced on a bright smile. 'Let's just say the night was fine — the morning not so much. We'll stick to purely business between us from now on.' She picked up her white, boxy handbag, perfect with today's neat blouse and slimline navy skirt. 'I'm heading off to St Ives to check out the shops and the Tate Gallery.'

'Good luck, and I expect to hear all about it later. At least I'll get some second-hand excitement.' Annie gave a wry smile. 'Come on, Jamie, we'll go and boil you an egg for your breakfast. Have a lazy day wandering around the shops.' She laughed good-naturedly as she headed for the stairs.

Tish didn't bother to contradict her, but she knew the hard work it had taken to get her business to this point, and the even harder continuing work it took to stay there. The sketch pad in her bag and her plan to tour the gallery would take precedence over shopping.

The warm sunny weather meant she

wouldn't need a jacket or umbrella. To her, the barely eighty-degree temperature was bliss, even if the Cornish thought they were in the middle of a heat wave. Mid-July in Nashville hovered around a hundred and dripped with humidity, so she determined to enjoy this day out and take her mind off the man with the devastating hands and lethal mouth. He'd confirmed all her suspicions last night by totally understanding her body, the same way he'd always seen through to her heart.

Enough. Stop it, you idiot.

She selected a bright, glossy carmine-red lipstick and applied it carefully, blotting with a tissue and then adding another layer. Tish swung her keys in her fingers and skipped down the stairs.

The forty-mile drive took about an hour on the slow, winding roads, but she mentally slowed as the distance increased between her and her problems. Rolling down the windows, she let in the warm scent of summer overlaid with the salty tang of coastal air.

Arriving at St Ives, she chose to park at the top of the hill and strode briskly down towards Porthmeor Beach and the Tate St Ives Gallery.

Tish stopped dead as the Tate came in sight, poised on a slope overlooking the sea. The pictures she'd checked out online didn't do justice to the large white building, starkly beautiful in the bright sunshine. At least she'd made one right decision today by coming here.

* * *

'You have to be joking.' Helena's chilly tones cut through Nico. 'You slept with the trashy American? Have you no taste?'

He didn't try to defend Tish or himself.

'I'm not sure what to say, Nico. I thought you were a man who appreciated a woman for more than her looks but obviously you're no different from the rest.' She snorted down the phone.

'A pair of overexposed breasts and your brain turns to mush.'

'I'm really sorry, Helena. I behaved appallingly.'

'Oh, Nico.' Her voice softened. 'We've been together a long time. I hate to throw it away because of one stupid mistake.'

He hated hearing Tish described as a stupid mistake, but what could he say? He and Helena had shared a safe, carefully controlled relationship for years, and the thought of losing that steady security filled him with unease.

'You'll have to give me the rest of the week to think about it.'

'Thank you. I don't deserve you,' he murmured.

'I'm not convinced yet,' she snapped. 'I'll call on Friday.'

She hung up and left him listening to an empty phone. If Helena forgave him, things must be over for good with Tish — no question. He shivered at the memory of Tish's hot, responsive body writhing under him and the exciting way in which she had burst into pleasure with one touch. He'd never experienced the same level of rightness with any other woman — but it transcended sex. Her parting words had hurt worse than being shot through the heart.

Before Friday he must make his own decision.

Nico stepped into his spare bedroom and opened the window. For a moment he simply breathed in the warm soft air before turning back around and mentally gearing up to work. He needed to finish two more paintings before the New York exhibition in January.

He glanced at the canvases propped up all around the room, dark images suffused with fire and anger, and his lingering sadness kicked back in. Years ago a therapist suggested he return to his love of art as an outlet for his guilt, but time wasn't healing his wounds and most days he thought he'd never exorcise the pain of losing his family.

Methodically he prepared his paints,

selecting the right brushes and changing the angle of the easel to catch the light better. No way was he good enough to capture Tish's image — her sleek, ebony hair was a life form in itself. He'd played with it in bed last night while she dozed, studying the texture and the colour, never quite able to pin it down. As for her creamy skin, could any artist capture its luminous nature?

Nico picked up his brush and started to paint.

Hours later he stood up to stretch and shook out his knotted-up shoulders. The light was changing, but when the art flowed this way he never wanted to stop. He glanced at his watch and realised it was late afternoon; his grumbling stomach told him he hadn't eaten, but the thought of food made him nauseous.

He wandered over to shut the window and a flash of black hair caught his eye. Nico pressed his hands against the glass.

Two sudden loud knocks on his front door startled him, and for a few seconds he considered not answering. It was probably a salesperson or the postman with a package, neither of which interested him. Slowly he walked out to the top of the stairs telling himself he was ridiculous to hope.

Seeing you again isn't on my agenda.

Two more loud knocks.

He ran downstairs and jerked open the door, taking a step backwards as Tish's fresh floral scent teased his senses.

'Don't say anything clever.' Her drawl shut him up before he could consider speaking. 'I'm only here to see if I left an earring behind. I was missing one when I got back home and intended to leave it, but it's one of my favourites.'

'I don't know. I . . . haven't cleared up.' He'd started to rip off the sheets earlier but hadn't been able to continue.

Tish planted her hands on her hips

and glared. Finally Nico realised she was waiting for him to invite her in. He stepped aside and she flounced past.

'I'll go and look. Stay here,' she ordered, heading upstairs.

Nico clasped his hands together, seeing the uncharacteristically untidy bedroom in his head. For the first time in at least a decade he hadn't made his bed.

She reappeared at the top of the stairs, her skin chalk-white. Faint lines creased her forehead.

'No luck?'

Tish waved the earring around and plastered on a wide, fake smile. 'Yep. It'd fallen off and slipped under the pillow — '

Her voice trailed away. Nico flinched, imagining how sick he'd have felt to discover it there tonight.

'Good.'

Tish walked quickly back down and stumbled on the last step. Automatically he opened his arms and she tripped right into them, giving a loud gasp as he held her tightly.

'Are you OK?' His raspy voice betrayed him. Desperately Nico cleared his throat. A faint blush tinged her creamy skin and she nodded. Without thinking he stroked his hand down over her heavy, silky hair, twisting it around his fingers.

'What went wrong this morning?' he whispered into her skin.

'You. Me. Helena. Too many years and too much baggage.' The words tumbled out, full of sorrow and regret.

'I know I'm not very expressive — '

'Understatement of the year,' she scoffed. 'You're the antithesis of the typical Italian.'

'I've had to be. You don't understand.' He loosened his hold on her, scared of the unsettling emotions she stirred in him.

'Help me to, Nico. You never told me what happened to your birth parents. Maybe it's time?' Her pale green eyes challenged him, but he shook his head.

'I can't.'

'Can't or won't?'

'You'd better go.' Nico forced out the words, part of him hoping she would refuse, but her sad, lingering glance told him he was chasing the moon.

'You're fooling yourself.' She shook her head gently.

'Maybe.' He dropped his arms. Stepping around him, Tish opened the door. Only when she was out in the street did she turn to say goodbye. When he made no reply she walked away.

Nico would push Tish back to the place in his mind where he needed her to stay . . . and then he'd be safe.

Idiot.

15

Unplugging her cell phone from the charger, Tish popped it in her bag. She'd planned out a route to take her travelling around Cornwall for a few days. It was divided between a selection of tourist haunts, which she hoped would inspire some new designs, and a number of vintage clothing shops she'd tracked down online. If work and clothes didn't put Nico from her mind, she was screwed.

The downside of this plan was the fact that it ate into her remaining time with Annie and Jamie — but at least there wasn't the disconcerting possibility of Nico De Burgh appearing around every corner.

She threw a baby-blue cardigan around her shoulders and headed down to the kitchen. 'I think I'm all set,' she declared.

'We'll miss you.' Annie glanced up from the stove where she was busy scrambling eggs and Jamie bounced in his highchair, banging his spoon. 'This one will too, won't you, sweetheart?'

Tish leaned down and ruffled her little brother's soft tufts of black hair, making him giggle even more delightedly.

'I'll be back on Wednesday.'

'Have a good time and remember to drive on the left,' Annie admonished.

'Yes, ma'am,' Tish said on purpose to watch her stepmother grimace. Annie had complained that being called 'ma'am' made her sound like an ancient old crone. 'I'm off.' She dropped a quick kiss on Jamie's head, avoiding his jam-smeared face and hands. 'Bye, poppet.'

She hurried from the house and for once, the car started first time. She made a last quick check of her map and turned on the radio to find a classic pop station to sing along with. At least, driving by herself, she wouldn't make anyone else's ears scream in pain at her tuneless warbling.

An hour later she found herself in Penzance but, instead of checking out the vintage clothing shop reputed to be the best in Cornwall, she was at the nearby head office of the Cornish Herald newspaper. A young reporter was happy to show her how skilled he was at tracking down old stories and obituaries. A short while later, she emerged clutching a handful of paper.

Tish wandered down the street and popped into the first coffee shop she found. Ordering a non-fat vanilla latte with two shots and hoping the caffeine boost would help her make sense of what she'd discovered, Tish tucked herself into a corner.

November 6, 1998. The coroner returned an open verdict in the death of Mrs Elaine Penwarren of The Breakers, Cliff Hill, Trevayne. Mrs Penwarren ingested a number of prescription medicines, but a verdict of suicide could not be proven.

Less than four months after she and her mother left for Nashville. Was there a connection? Tish spread out the next photocopied sheet and checked the date.

January 1, 1999. The coroner returned a verdict of death due to myocardial infarction on Mr William Penwarren of The Breakers, Cliff Hill, Trevayne.

Her heart shattered into a million pieces for Nico, who'd lost the only stability left in his life in two short months.

Tish sipped her coffee and thought hard. If he wouldn't tell her what happened to his real parents, she'd find out herself. Maybe then she'd understand, whether he wanted her to or not.

But she'd put this to one side until she had more time to think about her next move. Already she'd made enough rash decisions where Nico was concerned.

★ ★ ★

'Would it be alright if I stop by the house with some documents for you to sign, Mrs Treloare?' Nico asked. He could have sent them in the post, but he needed the possibility of seeing Tish. 'No, it's not inconvenient. I'll bring them over when I leave work, about half past five.'

He didn't even mind spending the rest of the afternoon working through an accumulated pile of boring paperwork. Gathering the completed files, he took them out to Josie.

'There you go. All ready to start on tomorrow.' He smiled and she looked surprised.

From nowhere a memory of his mother tickling him and making him laugh slammed into Nico, and he struggled to stay upright and breathing.

Abruptly he picked up his laptop case and headed for the door. 'I'm off. Good night.'

Josie gave him another curious look. Why? Didn't he usually say good night?

The warm early evening air hit him when he stepped outside and on impulse he pulled off his tie, opened the top button of his starched white shirt and rolled up the sleeves. He loved hot weather. He could do with a week sprawled out on a beach with nothing to do but work on his tan. Of course, that was if beautiful Tish was spread out next to him . . .

His mind did not need to go there. The sooner he accepted things could never work out between them, the better.

⋆ ⋆ ⋆

His heart thumped as he stood outside the door of number six, Beach Road and rang the bell.

'Oh — hello.' Annie gave him an exasperated look, her uncombed hair and lack of make-up indicating a bad day. She held a screaming Jamie under one arm, his legs flailing madly behind her. 'Go on into the kitchen. This monster's starving and isn't in the mood to wait.'

'I don't blame him.' Nico laughed.

'Right, well, come on.' Annie almost sprinted across the hallway and left him to follow. 'If you can find a spot, feel free to sit down.'

He moved a stack of clean washing from one of the chairs and cleared a space on the table, shoving a half-dead plant and a pile of discarded newspapers out of the way.

'I'm guessing your place is tidier?' Annie gave a wry smile.

'Well, yes, but it is only me . . . Tish thinks I'm finicky.'

Saying her name out loud sent a surge of heat through his body and Nico suspected he was blushing.

'Really.' She drew out the word, putting a lot more into it than a brief reply.

He watched in fascination as she juggled strapping Jamie into his high-chair and heating up something orange and mushy in the microwave, spooning it quickly into his open mouth.

'Tish isn't here.' She kept her attention on Jamie and Nico was relieved not to have to hide his disappointment.

'Oh. Right. Well, it was actually you I came to see.'

'I'm sure it was, Mr De Burgh. Doesn't the Royal Mail deliver in Trevayne these days?'

He cleared his throat. 'Please call me Nico. There's no need to be formal.'

'You frightened her off, you know.' Her shrewd eyes stared right at him and he flinched.

'Whatever do you mean?'

'Don't worry, she didn't go into any details, but it wasn't hard to guess. I bet you got all moral and high-handed.' She tossed the words out and carried on feeding Jamie. 'I expect you reminded her you have a girlfriend.'

'What if I did?' Nico didn't have a clue why he was defending himself to this inquisitive woman.

Annie put down the plastic spoon and said firmly, 'That was for you to remember *before* you talked Tish into bed.'

There was so much he could say but he dredged up a sliver of self-control from somewhere and held his peace.

'Fine.' Annie tossed her head. 'I know it's none of my business. Get the papers out for me to sign, and just in case you're interested, she won't be back until Wednesday.'

Nico refused to give Annie the satisfaction of asking where Tish was. He opened the envelope he'd brought, took out the five pages of documents, uncapped his gold-tipped ink pen and spread it all in front of her.

'She's driving around Cornwall working on a new ornament idea she's got.' Annie sounded proud of her new stepdaughter. 'She's got to be back in time for her dinner date with

Justin Coulthard, the marketing manager of the Tate St Ives, on Wednesday night. They got on well when she visited the gallery a few days ago and they're supposedly going to The Miner's Arms to discuss business.'

He wanted to wipe the satisfied smirk off Annie's face, but refused to let her see she'd needled him.

'Tish said he's very charming,' she continued.

Nico took back the papers she'd been signing and checked through them, willing his hands to remain steady.

'I hope she has a wonderful time.'

Liar. You'd rip Justin Coulthard limb from limb given a chance.

'I'd better be going.'

Jamie stared at him with Tish's light green eyes and for a second Nico's heart stopped. He stood up to leave.

'Sleep well tonight.' He patted the boy's spiky black hair and swallowed hard, thinking how one day it would resemble Tish's thick, heavy locks.

'Thanks. We need all the kind thoughts we can get in that direction.' Annie's warmth touched him and he managed to smile back. 'Tish was right,' she went on.

'In what way?'

'She told me you had an amazing smile, but I didn't believe her because I'd never seen it. You should use it more often, Nico, you might be surprised what an effect it'd have.'

He didn't answer, merely moved towards the door.

'See yourself out, if you don't mind,' she called after him and he caught a hint of laughter in her voice.

Nico escaped to his car. That had gone well. Not. He started the Alfa Romeo, jammed it into gear and sped away, taking the first curve far too fast. He fought through the red mist in his brain and forced his foot to hit the brake. He slowed down and drove the rest of the way at a steady speed, relieved to make it back to the garage unscathed.

Closing his front door behind him Nico headed straight for the grappa bottle and poured out a large measure before putting the bottle away. He turned on the TV and found a boring nature programme. Nothing on this should remind him of Tish.

16

Tish pushed open the front door with one hand, carrying her bags in the other. 'I'm back,' she called out cheerfully.

Annie appeared at the top of the stairs holding a warning finger up to her mouth. 'Shush. I've just got Jamie down. He barely slept last night and I'm about dead on my feet.'

'Sorry.'

Annie grinned. 'Go and put the kettle on. I've lots to tell you.'

Tish did as she was told and took down two of her favourite Cornish Blue pottery mugs from the cupboard. Annie must have been baking, because there were fresh oatmeal date bars in a plastic box on the counter.

'I don't expect they're up to your standards,' Annie joked, coming over to give Tish a hug and seeing her inspecting them.

'Oh, I'm sure they're delicious. You sit down, I'll bring it over.'

They sat quietly for a few minutes, drinking tea and munching happily. 'These are great,' Tish assured Annie.

Annie took another bar from the plate and gave a sly grin. 'Your moody Sicilian's been here moping around.'

'Nico? What for?'

'Supposedly to get me to sign some papers — but really he's pining over you,' Annie pronounced.

'Surely he didn't say so?' Tish couldn't get her head around that idea after the way they had parted.

'Well, no — but it didn't take a brain surgeon to work it out,' Annie said with certainty, stirring her tea.

No way was Tish going to encourage her stepmother's imagination. 'Enough of him,' she said firmly. 'Whatever there was between us is finished. Done. I need to go and get ready.'

She took her dishes to the sink. They rattled as her hands shook with a mixture of anger and longing.

'I don't think he liked the idea of you going out with the man from the gallery.'

Tish jerked around. 'How did he know about Justin?'

'I might've happened to mention your dinner date in passing.' Annie's lips twitched with obvious glee.

Inside Tish groaned, but tried to hide her annoyance.

'Oh well, no harm done. Anyway, I'm only meeting Justin to discuss a possible business opportunity.'

Annie rolled her eyes in disbelief. 'Right — is that what they're calling it these days? I'll clear up, but remember, I want to hear everything in the morning.'

Tish scoffed. 'There won't be much to report.' She sneaked quietly back upstairs to avoid waking Jamie.

Opening her bag, she pulled out the wonderful 1930s two-piece dress she'd found in a small shop in the backstreets of Redruth. Tish hung it up and sighed, imagining as she always did the woman who had worn this when it was new. It had probably been at an elegant cocktail party where a dashing man in evening dress played Noel Coward at the piano and everyone danced and laughed until the sun came up.

The black fabric was so sheer she'd need a slip underneath but, even with that, when she took off the short ruffled jacket it was a dress to make a man look more than once. If Nico intended to spy on her she'd give him something to watch.

* * *

Nico scowled into the dining room from his vantage point at the bar, his fingernails dug deep into his palms. How dare the man pick up one of Tish's hands and stare at her open-mouthed as though he wanted to eat her, as opposed to the food on their plates? He itched to go in there and land a punch right in the middle of

Justin Coulthard's model-boy-handsome face.

From deep in his pocket his mobile phone beeped and he dug it out to check the display. Helena. Nico turned the phone off. She could leave a message, and he'd listen when his brain cells weren't ravaged with jealousy.

'What the devil are you doing here?' Tish was standing inches from his face, her eyes flashing with fury.

Nico couldn't drag his gaze from her slim-fitting black dress, a swirl of delicate ruffles and lace hinting at so much more. His body tightened and he struggled to sound in control.

'I'm having a drink. People usually do in bars.' He shoved his hands in his trouser pockets and hastily pulled them out again, not wanting to draw attention to the painful arousal pressing against his fly.

'Don't lie.' She poked him in the chest and he grasped the edge of the bar stool to keep from toppling over as she caught him off-balance. 'Annie told you I'd be here.'

'She might've mentioned something.' He shrugged. 'I don't remember the details.'

Tish snorted. 'You remember everything.'

'Is something wrong?' The drawling, upper-class accent grated on Nico, but not as much as the way the big, blond man placed a hand on Tish's shoulder in a distinct signal of possession. 'Is this man bothering you?'

'I happen to be an old friend of Tish's and we were having a private conversation,' Nico snarled.

'We're not any more.' She attached herself to Coulthard's arm like a leech, but Nico caught the flash of surprise in the other man's eyes. A burst of satisfaction ran through his veins.

'I think you'd better leave.'

'I was just about to. I do apologise for interrupting. Enjoy the rest of your evening,' he snapped and headed out of the door before Tish could rip his head from his body.

The second he stepped outside Nico ripped off his tie and shrugged off his navy blazer, tossing it over one shoulder. He dodged traffic and wandering tourists to cross the road.

Leaning over the harbour wall, he sucked in a few steadying breaths of the warm evening air. The last boats were coming in for the night and he watched as the crews tied up and made things straight for the morning.

He turned his phone back on and it beeped with a voicemail alert. Pressing the button, he listened then slammed it shut, very tempted to throw it into the water.

'Now you've wrecked my night out, are you going to tell me what's going on?' Tish's voice startled him.

'Where's lover boy?' He glanced over her shoulder.

'Not that it's any of your business, but we're professional contacts, that's all. He's a very knowledgeable man about the arts and crafts scene in Cornwall. I shared some ideas I had about a new range of ornaments, and we discussed the possibility of selling them in the gift shop. End of story.'

'Always hold hands with colleagues, do you?' He shouldn't let her hear his bitterness, but the rage spreading through his body was consuming Nico beyond all sense.

Tish sighed, exasperation written all over her beautiful face. 'He was admiring my ring — it's one I designed myself. Nothing more. What do you want from me? Make up your mind.'

I want you in my bed. Naked.

'Come home with me so we can talk,' he pleaded. Nico didn't know how much he could bear to tell her, but he'd fought this with everything he had and still couldn't give up on her.

She folded her arms, tightening the gauzy material around her generous breasts. Nico's trembling hands pressed into his thighs as he struggled not to give in to the urge to grab her.

'Please, Tish.'

'Have you forgotten about the

precious Helena again? I wouldn't want to upset your wonderful little relationship.'

She tossed her hair back and it settled in a fall of silken temptation around her shoulders.

'There's nothing to upset,' he snapped. 'We're finished.'

'Since when?' she asked, full of curiosity.

He yanked out his phone. 'About twenty minutes ago.'

'Are you good with that?'

Nico met her fierce stare head on. 'Yes. Yes, I am.' He let go of the tension he'd clung onto since he got here and managed a tiny smile. 'So, are you coming?'

'Do you really think all you've got to do is tell me that it's over with the Ice Princess and I'll jump back in your bed?'

She sounded incredulous and he didn't blame her.

Nico touched his hand to her wrist, far too aware of her smooth, scented skin pulsing under his stroking fingers.

'I said I want to talk, and that's what I mean. Please, Tish.'

He watched her eyes soften and her defences crumble.

'Ok. You can give me a ride back to Trevayne. Justin offered, but I told him you're going that way anyway so I guess I'm stuck with you.'

Her voice was flat but Nico swore to make the most of what was on offer. He'd been given half an hour to change her mind.

★   ★   ★

Tish pressed herself as close to the car door as possible, wishing Nico wasn't wearing the same spicy cologne she remembered from their night together.

'I told Helena about us and she obviously wasn't happy.' He kept his gaze on the road but his jaw pulled so tight she was surprised it didn't crack. 'She wanted time to think. Earlier she left a message saying she thought it was

184

best we went our separate ways.'

'How did you reply?' Tish couldn't resist probing, her eyes drawn to the rigid set of his face.

'I didn't see it needed one.'

Tish laughed. 'Boy, for a smart man you can be dumb as a bag of rocks. You're supposed to call back and say you can't live without her, then she gets to cave in and forgive you.'

'How the hell did you work that out?' He sounded puzzled.

'I'm a woman. It's what we do.' Sometimes she pitied clueless men. 'No way could she let you get away with this too easily. The secret is to torment you just long enough, and then give in with the right amount of reluctance so that you feel thoroughly guilty for a very long time.'

Nico shook his head, obviously bewildered. 'And what if I don't want to?'

His serious, steady words took her by surprise.

'Don't you?'

Out of the blue he put on his indicator and pulled over. He gripped the steering wheel so hard that the veins in his hands stood at attention.

'No,' Nico declared in a no-nonsense tone. 'No, I don't.'

'Right.' This was the time to choose her words carefully. 'Would you feel the same way if I wasn't around?'

Was that vain? she wondered.

Nico picked up her right hand, playing with the fingers and saying nothing. His gaze moved to her mouth and he leaned closer, the pulse throbbing in his neck. The searing heat rising from his body wrapped around her and Tish gasped for breath. His hand slid around the back of her neck and pulled her to him. As his probing tongue teased at her lips she moaned from deep in the back of her throat.

Logic . . . answers to her questions . . . nothing mattered but the taste of him, and she couldn't get enough. He plundered her mouth, taking everything and leaving her powerless to resist. Nico tortured her until she came close to screaming, then withdrew to plant light kisses all over her mouth.

He eased away and fixed her with a fierce, hungry gaze.

'You *are* here.' Nico's long, firm fingers thrust up into her mane of hair, shameless in his explorations. 'Oh, you always smell so wonderful. You must bathe in sunlight.'

'That's a bit poetic for a sensible lawyer, isn't it?' Tish struggled for some last remnant of commonsense.

'It's the effect you have on me. What can I say?' A smile creased his face, taking years off him.

'You're not the only one,' she whispered, deciding in a single, blinding second to take a chance. 'Drive as fast as possible back to your place. You can make love to me first, drive me crazy by seducing me with all the romantic Italian words you know — but afterwards we're going to have the talk we've needed to have for a very long time.'

His liquid brown eyes melted any last

resistance she had.

'I believe I can obey your instructions, amore mio, my love.'

'Good. Now drive.' She leaned back in the seat, her heart racing and her whole body tingling with anticipation.

17

'Yes, Mrs Penlee, I agree. We do need the rubbish collected every week. Would you like me to contact our councillor?' Nico held on to his thin thread of patience as he listened to his neighbour's complaints. She'd popped out of her house, watering can in hand, as soon as he and Tish walked up the street after parking the car.

'You'm a good boy. You tell them we pay our taxes and they can't get away with cutting back, especially in the summer.' The woman's beady eyes hadn't stopped examining Tish the whole time she spoke.

'By the way, do you know Tish Carlisle? You'd remember her as Patricia Treloare.' He made the introductions and grinned in spite of himself as Tish turned on her hundred-watt smile.

'Course I do. You and my Debbie

were up at Polgreen School together, weren't you?'

'Yes, ma'am. How's she doing?'

The woman's face darkened. 'She be living up Roche way. Can't afford nothing down here. She's married and got two kiddies — with another on the way.' A smile lit up her face as she spoke about her grandchildren.

'That's wonderful.'

Nico noticed Tish's jaw tighten, unsure whether it was with horror or jealousy.

'You've turned into a right pretty girl, although you do talk like one of them Yanks. I'm surprised some man's not snatched you up before now.'

Tish chuckled. 'He'd have to be fast to catch up with me. I've got my own business and it's my priority.'

A tiny streak of disappointment ran through Nico. Did she mean that, or was she just quashing Mrs Penlee's nosiness?

'This one's a handsome one — you could do worse.' She pointed at Nico and he winced.

'Between you and me, I agree — but don't tell him,' Tish said in a stage whisper, her eyes sparkling with mischief.

'We mustn't hold you up from seeing to your flowers. They're always so beautiful.' Nico gestured over at the hanging baskets full of colourful geraniums. 'We have some business to discuss, if you'll excuse us.'

'You run along and remember to talk to that rogue of a councillor. Remind him who elected him in the first place.'

'I will, Mrs. Penlee. Good night.' Firmly Nico steered Tish away before she could get involved in any more incendiary conversations.

He unlocked the door and pushed her inside, slamming it shut behind them with his foot.

'Business to discuss?' She grinned, hands on hips, her breasts straining against the black lace. 'What kind of business would that be, Mr De Burgh?'

Nico grabbed her shoulders, shoving her back against the wall. He delved his tongue between her parted lips and revelled in her sweetness. Sliding his hands down, he grasped her rear and moved a knee between her legs, pressing them apart. 'See what you've done to me.' He ground his steely arousal against her and rotated his hips, mimicking what he intended to do next.

'Oh, God, Nico, Don't stop. Do it here. Now.' She groaned and shoved her hands up through his hair, driving his last remnant of sense out the window.

He seized the ruffled hem of her dress and pushed it up around her waist. His heart thumped at the sight of the scrap of black lace barely covering her soft curls.

'Pretty . . . but it's got to go.' He ripped off the panties and grinned lustfully. 'Much better.' He slid one finger hard into her and she clenched around him, moaning.

'Make me come. Hard,' she gasped and pulsed against him as he went deeper, adding another finger. Her eyes widened and glazed over as he hit the perfect spot, sending her over the edge. He held her up as she slumped against him, quivering, then let go with one hand and searched frantically in his pocket.

'Let me.' Tish, desperate for more, snatched the foil packet from his hand and ripped it open with her teeth. 'What're you waiting for?' she teased.

Nico unzipped his trousers in one swift move, pushed the fabric aside and freed himself. She ran her fingers lightly down over him and Nico groaned, desperate to be inside her. He thrust into her hand as she took care of business.

'You know what to do next,' Tish teased and rested back against the wall, her eyes burning with pure passion.

'Slide your legs up around me. I'll hold you,' Nico growled and she wrapped them around his waist, breathing hard as he held himself ready. With one passionate thrust he sunk into her depths and she took him easily, all the way.

'Hold on,' he gasped raggedly. 'This won't be gentle.'

'Good.'

He pulled almost all the way out and plunged back in again, deeper than before. Tish moved in synch with him, her eyes never leaving his face.

'Harder. Don't be nice.' She urged him on, making him mindless with wanting.

'Nice? I'm way past that, gorgeous.' He slammed into her over and over and Tish screamed, convulsing around him and sending Nico tumbling into his own explosive release. Her nails dug into his back under his shirt.

'Are you still alive?' Nico murmured into the curve of her neck, sucking at the soft, sweet skin.

'I think so. You?' She smiled and touched his face, stroking over his lips and down to his jaw.

'Maybe.' He eased out of her body and gently let down her legs, holding onto her waist as her feet touched the floor.

'Do you want to get dressed, or go up to my bedroom?' he asked hopefully.

Tish rested a hand on his cheek. 'We agreed we'd talk. I know we'd both rather . . . '

'Have more fun?'

'Yeah, but . . . '

He caressed her hair, playing with the black, silky heaviness. 'I could make love to you all day and night.' Sighing, he dropped his hands to his thighs. 'But of course, you're right.'

He straightened up his clothes as he spoke, and bent down to pick up her destroyed panties, passing them back to her with a rueful smile. 'Not sure these are much good. Sorry.' He didn't sound in the least bit apologetic and she smiled right back.

'I've got more. It was worth it.'

He waited while she pulled her dress back into place and took hold of her hand to lead her into the living room. Without speaking, they sat on the sofa and he wrapped his arm around her shoulder.

'Where do you want me to start?' he asked.

'What happened to make you come here in the first place?'

'Pick the easiest thing, why don't you?'

He never spoke about his family to anyone. The Penwarrens had tried getting him to open up when he first arrived, but gave up when he politely refused all their approaches. Tish deserved the complete truth, but he hoped the small part he could make himself share would satisfy her.

'I lost all my family in an accident.' Nico closed his eyes, his head filled with the fierce explosion, the fire and the screams. He clasped his hands, desperate to stop the shivers running through his body. 'I still can't talk about it. I'm sorry. I thought maybe I could with you. Perhaps one day.'

His words trailed away, and one glance at Tish revealed disappointment written right across her face.

'William Penwarren was an old friend of my father's. They were at university together in London.' He chose his words with extreme care. 'It wasn't safe for me to stay in Sicily, so my uncle arranged for me to come here.'

'What do you mean — not safe?' She picked on the one word he shouldn't have uttered.

'I . . . can't explain, not exactly.' Nico stroked her soft cheek and she leaned into his touch. 'I'm sorry, Tish.'

'Were you in the accident too?' Tish's quiet sympathy made his throat tighten. He didn't deserve her kindness. If he hadn't been so difficult, his family might still be alive — or he'd be dead along with them. Many days he had wished that he was.

'No.' He shifted so that he wasn't touching her any more, but she didn't let him get away with that and pressed his hand.

'You blame yourself?' She scrutinised him so fiercely that he couldn't look away. 'You do, don't you?'

Nico's voice refused to work. He dropped his head to his chest but Tish's fingers slid under his chin and pushed gently, forcing him to look up. Tears glistened in her eyes. One escaped and out of instinct he brushed it away. She seized his hand.

'I don't know the details, but I'm sure your parents would hate to see you doing this to yourself.'

'You don't understand. I killed them.'

She flinched at his harsh words but still she held onto him. Why didn't she hate him?

Tish's small laugh shocked him. 'Don't be ridiculous. You're too smart to believe that crap, and so am I.'

Nico jerked out of her grasp and stood up. 'You know nothing except what I've told you.'

She jumped up too and held her hand over his heart. All he wanted was to lose himself in her again, push the demons away.

'Oh, my love.' Her voice broke and

she kissed his cheek with such tender-
ness he almost cracked. To share the
burden would be such a relief, but at
the last second he couldn't. It almost
killed him to do it, but he pushed her
away.

18

Nico's taut body, closed-down face and impenetrable eyes all made it clear he wouldn't be easily coaxed. Tish needed to back off for now and wait until his defences were down again.

'How about we leave it for now?' she said artlessly, and his sceptical lawyer's stare brought her close to laughter. 'We'll talk more when you feel like it, but I hope you don't take too long because I'm leaving next week. I need to get back for the Las Vegas trade show. It's a big one and makes a huge difference in orders for next year.'

His eyes darkened to the shade of burnt molasses and she pressed on, determined to give him something more to think about. 'I've already stayed longer than planned and my staff are getting antsy.'

'Do you enjoy that side of the

business?' he asked with a rare touch of diffidence.

'Not really. It's essential, but I'd rather be designing.'

'Can't someone else take over that stuff for you?'

Was he asking because he wanted her to stay, or out of concern for her well-being?

'They could, but my partner, Sadie, and I have shared the responsibility since the business took off and it's hard to make changes. At some point I need to rethink everything.'

She allowed the thought to hang between them and small frown lines appeared between his eyes.

'If I want to focus on designing, I need to separate myself from the marketing side of the business. At the moment I feel I'm not doing either to the absolute best of my ability.'

'Is that what you were discussing with Coulthard?' Nico shook his head in disgust. 'Stupid me. Barrelling in there and acting as if I was your keeper.'

'Yeah, it was — but you weren't to know.' Tish succumbed to a big grin. 'I know it's a bit teenage-girly but it gave me a kick to see you jealous.'

'I — ' He gave up the pretence and nodded.

'It's alright to admit you're human.' Tish took a risk and slid her arms up around his neck, toying with his thick, dark hair. His hot, hard mouth seized on hers and he teased her relentlessly with his tongue until she opened to him. Boy, the man could win an Olympic gold medal for kissing.

Out of the blue he pulled away.

'What's going to happen to us?'

The sadness behind his tortured eyes shook her to the core.

'I don't know. Don't ask me today. Please.' She yearned to push it all away for a while. Tish cupped his face in her hands, rubbing her fingers over the dark stubble shading his jawbone. She ached for him to rub his face against her soft skin, all over, marking her as his. 'Give me this, Nico.'

'I've never been able to refuse you.' He plundered her mouth with another devastating kiss. 'Bed?'

Tish signalled her answer with a nod, then an excited squeak as Nico's strong arms swept her off her feet.

'I intend to take my time for once,' he growled, nipping at her neck, licking and sucking the tender skin.

'Not too long, I hope,' she teased.

'As long as I want — and you'll love it,' he declared with an evil grin.

She made a half-hearted protest out of a lifetime habit of rebellion.

'Ah, my Tish, always feisty.' He kissed the top of her head. 'Let's enjoy each other and not worry about tomorrow.'

Nico's soft words wrung her heart and she rested her head in the crook in his shoulder. It was her way of surrendering, and he gave her such a look of gratitude that she found herself fighting back tears.

He carried her easily across the room but, as he put his foot on the bottom step, the telephone rang.

'Ignore it,' Tish murmured against his neck.

'I'd better get it.' He eased her back down on her feet. 'Go on up and I'll join you in a minute.'

Tish nodded but didn't move as he walked quickly towards the phone.

Nico snatched it up. 'Yes.' His brain struggled to catch up at the sound of his uncle Antonio's voice. Out of practice, it took a few seconds to click back into Italian mode.

'No, I'm not planning to visit any time soon. You know why.'

He listened to his uncle's standard line of persuasion, the usual story of how it would do him good to face the past. According to him, the danger to Nico was minimal these days since they'd locked up the thugs who murdered his family five years earlier. A couple of times a year Antonio made the same call and Nico gave the same answers. He held it together until his uncle's voice cracked speaking his beloved sister's name.

'I can't. I'm sorry,' he snapped and hung up, planting his hands on the table for a moment to steady them, willing his ragged breath back under control.

'Is everything alright?'

He jerked around to meet Tish's curious eyes. Why couldn't the damn woman ever do what she was told? Now he had to lie some more. 'It's fine.'

'Then why have you gone a funny shade of green as though you're going to throw up all over your expensive rug?'

'You're exaggerating, cara, Tish.' He struggled to sound cool and unconcerned.

'Not this time.' She walked towards him, her hands on hips, glaring so hard that he almost gave in. She'd forced him out of his serious, closed-down shell when he was a teenager, and if he wasn't careful she'd do it again. 'Who was calling? I recognise Italian when I hear it.'

'It's private business. I'm not discussing it today.'

205

The sooner he ended this foolish relationship with Tish, the better it would be for them both, he thought savagely. Peter was right all along. With the burden of his family's tragic accident always at the back of his mind, he'd pushed away the awful knowledge of why his foster mother died. He couldn't betray the Penwarren family any longer, no matter how much he desired the beautiful woman gazing at him with puzzled intensity.

'I'm sorry — but maybe it's as well this happened.'

'How'd you work that one out?' she retorted, her face flaming with angry heat.

'We can't pretend the last thirteen years haven't happened. We've both moved on and changed.'

A complete lie, because moving on was the one thing he was totally unable to do.

'I should hope so!' Tish fired straight back. 'I don't want to be the same confused, rebellious girl I was, and I'm

206

sure you don't want to be the same sullen, mixed-up boy either.' Her face softened and she touched his arm. 'I kinda like the man you've turned into and I thought you felt the same about me?'

He hated the hurt lingering behind her eyes, and himself for putting it there. Unable to resist, Nico cupped her face with his hands, stroking his thumbs over her silky skin.

'You don't understand and I can't explain. You have to accept things as they are . . . or leave.'

'Whatever are you talking about?'

Nico dropped his hands down to his sides and in a cold, deliberate way closed down his heart. 'My relationship with Helena worked because she didn't ask questions about certain aspects of my life. You don't know how to be that way.'

'No, I don't. Maybe you should go back to her,' she snarled.

'Perhaps I will.'

Tish's hand flew up to cover her

mouth but a gulping sob escaped and she stumbled backwards. 'I feel sorry for you. You're going to have an empty life.'

He grimaced as her words sliced through him, but he remained silent. Tish snatched up her handbag from where she'd tossed it on the floor earlier and ran for the door. As she flung it open she turned. 'Be very sure, Nico. I won't be back.'

He held perfectly still and Tish's face crumpled as she realised he meant what he said.

'Bastard.' She spat out the single word and ran out, slamming the door behind her.

Now he was alone again. He'd got what he asked for.

★ ★ ★

The yellowy lights from the Blue Anchor gleamed around the next corner and Tish picked her way across the uneven cobblestones. She'd go in and have a drink to calm down before she headed back up Beach Road.

Five minutes later, she was tucked away in the back corner of the pub nursing a double Scotch. She replayed the last few hours in her head. How could Nico be driven to distraction with passion one minute and cold as ice the next?

'It's little Patricia, isn't it?' A ruddy-faced older man pulled out the other chair at the small table. 'You don't recognise me, do you?' He smiled, revealing several missing teeth.

'Should I?' Tish looked closer but nothing clicked. She wished he'd leave her alone.

'Percy Walker. Uncle Percy?'

Tish stared in shock. 'Oh, my goodness, I don't believe it.' Her focus switched from the man's lined, weathered face to his sparkling green eyes and laughing mouth. Imagining black hair on the bald head helped, and instantly she was a child again. 'How have you been keeping — and how's Aunty Marge?'

His smile faded. 'The wife passed away five years ago. Heart.' He took a deep swallow of beer and studied her.

Tish swallowed hard. 'I'm sorry.'

'That's life, my dear. You go on. Not much choice.'

He's right, she thought with fresh resolve. She'd never given up before and wouldn't start now.

'*He* were right proud of your ornament business.'

'Really? His new wife wasn't sure he knew.'

Percy's hooded eyes darkened. 'He didn't talk about the past much in front of her, but he did to me. We'd meet for a pint most Friday nights. I miss him.'

Tears pressed at Tish's eyes. She missed her father too, but it had taken coming here to admit it to herself.

'I won't keep you now, my dear — I've got a darts match to play.'

'I'd love to hear some more about my dad. I'll be here another week, so maybe I'll see you in here another night?'

Percy Walker patted her hand. 'It'll be my pleasure, dear. I'm in most evenings around now.'

Tish nodded and watched him go, hot tears pressing at her eyes. She'd arrived emotional and upset and was leaving the same way. Not exactly an improvement.

19

'Is that you, Tish?' Annie's cheery voice called out from the kitchen. 'Come in and dish the dirt on your evening.'

'I'm coming.' She sucked in a calming breath and plastered on a smile. Tish didn't rush, but it only took half a dozen slow steps to cross the hall and stand in the kitchen door.

'Hi . . . I thought you'd be in bed by now?'

'Hmm. Judging by your fake cheerfulness, I'd say things didn't go well with Mr Coulthard.'

Annie's shrewd eyes bored into her and Tish cringed. This woman was as hard to fool as her own mother.

'Sit down and I'll pour you some coffee. I know you prefer it to tea, although you're too polite to complain.'

Tish shut her mouth on the protest she'd started to make and took the mug from Annie's outstretched hand. Only when she'd drunk half of the hot, strong brew did she consider speaking again.

'Thanks. I needed that.'

'I thought you might.' Annie pulled out a chair and sat down to join her. 'Jamie went down early tonight so I indulged in a couple of glasses of wine while I watched the dancing programme.'

Tish managed a smile. 'I'm glad. You deserve a break.'

'Now we've got past the pleasantries tell me what happened. Did Justin make a move on you? I told you he would.'

That part of the evening seemed so long ago that Tish strained to remember. 'No, for once you're wrong. We chatted about work and I floated a few design ideas I have. If things work out they might pick up a range of ornaments.'

'Great — so why the sour look?' Annie pinned her down.

'Three guesses who turned up at the restaurant?' Her new stepmother frowned. 'Mr De Burgh himself.'

'Oh.' Annie blushed and glanced away.

'Yeah, 'oh'. Cutting a long story short he gave me a lift back here and I was stupid enough to succumb to his charms before being dumped — again. Sound familiar? It's a habit I intend to break.' She couldn't hide her bitterness.

'I'm sorry.'

'It's not your fault. I'm old enough to have more sense. Just because he's hot and . . . ' Tish's voice faded. Memories of Nico's glorious body plundering hers sent a rush of heat up her neck to set her face on fire. Were they doomed to be one of those couples who only connected in bed? She didn't really believe it, but the hurt eased slightly to think so.

Annie squeezed her hand, and her sympathy made Tish's eyes prickle with tears. 'Anyway. Whatever it was or wasn't is over.' She struggled to be sensible. 'I've got a lot to think about apart from him, and decisions to make — plus I need to be in Las Vegas by next Tuesday.'

Picking up the coffee pot, Annie refilled Tish's mug and selected another biscuit from the tin on the table. 'You're being too hard on yourself. Don't beat yourself up for being human. I held it all in for days after your father died, but do you know what broke me?'

Tish shook her head. If she even tried to speak she'd burst into tears.

'His toothbrush.' Annie swallowed hard. 'The sight of his toothbrush in the bathroom. Knowing he'd never need it again. I sat on the toilet lid and cried for hours.'

'I . . . It's everything. Dad. Nico. Work. I've always been strong and I don't understand why all of a sudden I'm not.' Tish's voice faded to a whisper and Annie gave her a small smile.

'My theory is, we can only take so much before exploding. My mother saw the state I was in so she took Jamie and me home with her for a week. I'm not saying it was easy being there, or coming back again afterwards, but I could handle it better.' She hesitated a second before carrying on. 'I've got an idea.'

'Go on.'

'My sister, Babs, lives in Boscastle on the north coast. She's got a couple of spare rooms and does bed and breakfast for visitors. We were on the phone earlier and she was moaning about someone cancelling at the last minute. It's a beautiful area and near Tintagel where King Arthur's supposed to have lived. It'd be an ideal place to inspire your designs.'

'Are you sure it'd be alright?' Tish was uncertain.

'I'll ring her now, if you like.'

'Isn't it too late?'

Annie laughed and shook her head. 'If I give you a chance to think too much, you'll wriggle out of it.' She picked up her mobile and Tish listened, bemused, as the conversation jumped from her proposed visit to Jamie's brilliance and the escalating price of bread. Annie closed the phone and gave her a satisfied grin.

'All set. She's expecting you before lunch tomorrow and she'll put you up for three nights. It's not that I'm trying to get rid of you, but you could head straight to London from there. It'd save you from the possibility of meeting up with you-know-who.'

'Yes, ma'am.' Tish gave a mock salute.

'And before you have to ask, I won't tell our sexy solicitor where you are.'

Tish grabbed her hands tightly. 'Thanks. I'd better go and get some sleep.' A forlorn hope, but she'd make the effort to pretend. 'It's been a long day to say the least.' She stood up and headed for the door.

She'd prove she could do without Nico De Burgh in her life.

★   ★   ★

Nico half-dozed on the sofa and startled awake as someone banged on his front door. His heart raced, praying it was Tish giving him yet another chance. He opened the door and his face tightened with disappointment.

'Peter? What the devil are you doing here?'

The man he considered his brother broke into a grin and punched him on the arm.

'Nice greeting, I'm sure. I'm glad I travelled five thousand bloody miles to see you.' He pushed a computer bag into Nico's arms and picked up the suitcase at his feet. 'You going to ask me in?'

'Sorry. You took me by surprise, that's all. You've never dropped in unannounced from California before.' Nico stood back to let him in. 'Come on.'

Ten minutes later, in the kitchen, Nico poured out two mugs of freshly ground coffee and stared at Peter, stunned by the story he'd just been told. 'You're kidding me.'

'Nope. Aunt Marlene gave me the letters a couple of days ago. I nearly rang you, but phoning struck me as wrong.'

'You've brought them with you?'

'No, dummy, I left them all at home.' Peter chuckled and opened up his computer bag to pull out a large brown envelope.

'Cool it. Aunt Marlene was going through Uncle Jack's papers in his study and found these in the back of a cupboard. Apparently Dad wrote every week after Jack emigrated.' He opened the flap and shook out a stack of thin, blue airmail letters onto the table. 'Most are full of the usual dull stuff — where he's been, the weather and so on.' He rifled through and pushed half a dozen letters towards Nico. 'These are the ones you'll be interested in. Read them in date order.'

Nico picked up the first and studied the outside.

'It's not going to blow up in your face.' Peter jested then his smile disappeared. 'Oh, damn. I didn't mean to — '

'It's ok. There's no need to tiptoe around — I'm not a kid.'

Not that it made much difference. Even now he couldn't watch an explosion on the news or in a film without flinching or wanting to run away and hide.

'I shouldn't have been so bloody thoughtless. Sorry,' Peter persisted, seeing the pain in his face.

'Put a sock in it and let me read.' Nico opened out the delicate paper and the sight of William Penwarren's flowing, black script made his heart clench. The hours his foster father had spent teaching him to write in English were engraved in his mind; he'd have been so proud to see Nico become a lawyer.

He forced himself to start reading. The first paragraphs were unremarkable but in one sentence it all changed.

Something's going on with Elaine but she won't talk to me about what's wrong. Some days she doesn't get out of bed and when she does, she doesn't bother to wash or get dressed properly. I'm doing everything around the house but she doesn't notice or seem to care. I suggested going to the doctor but she screamed at me. She's scaring me; I don't know what to do.

'Do you remember Mum being ill?' Nico frowned. 'I don't.'

Peter nodded. 'You were still having a hard time settling in with us.'

'In other words I was too wrapped up in myself to notice?'

'Don't be harsh on yourself. Remember, I was older so I was more aware. Read the next one.'

Reluctantly Nico did as he was told.

You'll say I'm paranoid, Jack, but I think Elaine's got another man. All of a sudden she's dressing up every day and putting on make-up. She disappears from the house for hours and won't say where she's going.

He tossed it to one side before picking up the following week's letter in which William admitted he'd followed Elaine and seen her meet Frank Treloare.

'I don't get it. Earlier you implied you'd found proof Frank wasn't to blame for what happened to Mum?'

'Don't jump to conclusions,' Peter warned.

'Seems pretty clear to me.'

Peter seized the pile of letters and searched through, passing one to Nico. 'Read this one. It's dated a month after Dad went to fetch her from the Treloares' house.'

I found out yesterday why Elaine's been so erratic. She's seriously ill, but couldn't bear to tell me. The medicine they put her on gave her severe mood swings. She couldn't help herself, Jack. Elaine says there's nothing they can do and by Christmas I'll be bringing up two boys alone.

Peter rested a comforting hand on his shoulder. 'He goes on to make it clear Frank didn't know about Mum's illness. He was unhappy in his marriage and really loved her. Dad shouldn't have made us promise to stay away from the Treloares. It wasn't fair.'

'He was devastated. People do irrational things.' Nico struggled to understand.

'If you and Tish have something worthwhile, don't let the past stop you.'

Nico grimaced. 'We aren't even speaking now. I didn't treat her right.' He gestured towards the letters. 'Thanks for bringing these, though. It gives me some peace of mind. You're not running off back to California straight away, are you?'

'I'll stay a few days.' Peter gave him a sly grin. 'Maybe you should consider showing these to Tish?'

'Don't be a moron,' Nico protested. 'I'm sure she doesn't know about the affair.'

'Maybe she does, but won't mention it either. You're probably one as daft as the other.'

Nico didn't reply. Grown-up Tish wasn't a woman to hold back on anything; he was pretty sure she'd have challenged him before now if she knew of their parents' liaison.

'Keep the letters in case you change your mind. I made copies and left them back home with Karen. I'll shut up now. Show me your spare bed, and I'll crash for the night. I'm shattered.'

'How about you take my bed and I'll make do with the sofa?' Nico suggested.

'You don't have a guest room?'

'Well, yes, but it's sort of . . . full.'

Peter stood and picked up his bag. 'I don't mind a mess. I'm knackered. Show me the room and leave me to zone out for about ten hours straight.'

Unless Nico's brain came up with something in the next thirty seconds, he'd be forced to make explanations he'd successfully avoided for a very long time.

20

Striding across the bedroom, Nico flung a cover over Tish's portrait as Peter walked through the door.

'You sly old devil. I thought you'd given up this lark years ago.' His brother glanced around at the paintings stacked against the wall and on easels.

'No, I never did.' Nico met his inquisitive stare and sighed. 'It keeps me this side of sane.'

Peter nodded and moved in to study them more closely. 'Bit dark, aren't they?'

Nico shrugged. There wasn't really an answer to that.

'You ever thought of trying to sell any? Karen dragged me to some art museum last time we were in LA and these remind me of a couple I saw there.'

Peter glanced down at the signature in the right-hand corner and all the colour left his face. '*Enigma*. My God, they were yours, weren't they? What's with the name thing, little brother?'

'It's not a big deal. I'd rather stay anonymous, that's all. Drives my agent crazy, but . . . ' He tried to smile but didn't feel it reach his eyes. 'I prefer not to have my real name shouted around and have the whole story of my family dragged out and plastered across the tabloids. I couldn't take it.'

His voice broke and he was forced to walk away and stare out of the window, taking deep breaths in an effort to steady down.

Peter's strong hand clasped his shoulder but Nico couldn't turn around.

'I get it. Don't worry. Your secret's safe with me.'

'Thanks,' he mumbled.

'So is this the one you're working on now?'

Before Nico could stop him Peter yanked the cover away, revealing Tish's almost complete portrait. Her beseeching, pale green eyes met his and a shard of pain cut right through his heart. His brother let out a long, low whistle.

'You didn't tell me she turned into such a beauty. Last time I saw her she was a scrawny kid mooning around after you,' Peter recalled with a chuckle. 'You're a bloody idiot to let her go because of your damn Sicilian pride.'

'It's all I have left,' Nico whispered.

Peter swung around, his eyes dark with anger.

'Don't be an idiot. I might be crossing the line saying this, but I think your parents would be ashamed to hear you say such a dumb thing. You're a successful solicitor and an accomplished artist. You're not short of money and you've had to beat women off with a stick ever since you stopped being a gawky teenager. So what's your problem? You're not the only person who ever grieved over people they loved, you know.'

Nico flinched, his brother's words slapping him as surely as if he'd used his hand.

'Don't hold back, please, feel free to smack me down some more,' he snapped.

'You don't need anyone else's sympathy, you give yourself enough to wallow and drown in.'

Peter's tight, red face betrayed his disgust. One wrong word on Nico's part and their relationship might not recover from this. He couldn't lose this man, too.

Nico took a step away and raised his hands in a gesture of surrender. 'Hey, take it easy. I know I'm an idiot but we all have bad habits. Get some sleep and we'll talk more in the morning.'

'You sure about that — or will you close down again?'

He could give an easy answer, he supposed, but it would be seen right through.

'I honestly don't know. No one's ever tried to make me before, except for — '

'Tish? Thought so. Women always see too much.' Peter's wry smile dragged an answering one from Nico against his will. 'I'm going to bed before I drop. Think about what I said.'

* * *

Despite all the problems that filled Tish's brain, the immediate one which needed solving was what to wear this morning. She flicked through the clothes she'd brought and decided, in the absence of anything remotely medieval and Arthurian, it'd have to be her Seventies hippy-style multi-coloured skirt combined with a white peasant blouse and leather thong sandals. Tish added a handful of thin silver bracelets and a cowbell necklace before finishing off with a floral headband.

She checked the effect in the mirror and decided it would do. In a few minutes, her packing was finished and she collected all her bags and ran downstairs.

'You are going to Boscastle, not Woodstock, you know!' Annie teased, admiring her outfit while she balanced Jamie on one hip. 'Are you all set?'

'I think so.' Tish dropped her luggage on the floor and took a step closer to rest her hand on Jamie's soft, black hair. 'I don't know if I'll . . . ' She choked back tears, unable to squeeze the words from her aching throat.

'It's ok. Go and do what you need to. You'll be back,' Annie stated with such sureness that Tish's heart lifted.

'Yeah, I will — and soon.' She met Annie's kind eyes and pulled her into a hug. 'I know why my father loved you and I'm glad he was happy in the end.'

Jamie wailed as they squeezed him between them and Annie gently eased away. She murmured soothing words and glanced at Tish over his shoulder. 'Go on, before we flood the house out between us. Drive carefully and give Babs our love.'

It was lucky that one of them had willpower; Nico had sucked all hers away. 'I will. Take care of yourself and this sweet boy.' Tish dropped another kiss on Jamie's head but he wriggled away, making her laugh.

'I'm off.' Quickly she picked up her bags and headed for the door, not daring to stop until she reached the safety of her car.

She entered her destination in the GPS and started the engine. An hour of concentrating on driving should ready her for a new challenge — proving she didn't need Nico De Burgh.

★ ★ ★

'Come in, my dear, I'm Babs.' An older, plumper version of Annie, with the same sharp blue eyes, greeted Tish. 'I'll show you your room then leave you alone unless you ask for company. Annie gave me instructions,' she said with a laugh.

'I'm sure she did. I'll be out a lot, but when I am around I'd sure like to get to know you. I'm not planning on being a hermit.' Tish grinned, the first time she'd felt like doing so for days.

'Good. My pesky sister says I only take in guests because I'm nosey.' Babs shrugged. 'Actually she's right.'

'At least you're honest.' Tish picked up her bags and Babs headed up the stairs, leaving her to follow.

'I've given you the front room. It's got the best view.'

'That's great, thank you. How far is Tintagel from here?'

'Only about three miles, dear. Are you into all the King Arthur nonsense?'

Tish laughed. 'I'm guessing you're not?'

The other woman scoffed and busied herself straightening the bright red and white flowery curtains.

'It intrigues me and I hope to get some design ideas for my business,' Tish went on.

'Christmas ornaments, Annie said. Odd way to make a living but she says you're good.'

Unsure if she'd been complimented or not, Tish nodded.

'I'll leave you to it.' Babs left and Tish

was drawn towards the window.

Today's sky was a perfect, clear blue and she could make out the glittering sea not far away, over across a couple of fields. Unpacking could wait. Tish picked up the small, canvas bag with her drawing supplies and threw in her keys, phone and purse.

Last night when she couldn't sleep she'd read up all about Tintagel. She vaguely remembered coming here with her parents as a child. Her father lured her with a book of legends all about King Arthur and the knights of the Round Table and she'd lapped it all up.

With the current craze for all things fantasy and mystical this should be a cinch to sell — romantic and other-worldly. Not typical for Christmas, but a sliver of excitement ran through Tish at the thought of creating something completely different. She hadn't felt this much excitement over a design idea for a long time.

Half an hour later, she parked close to the rugged headland and walked across to the castle ruins. Finding a convenient rock to sit on just off the path she got out her sketch pad, relishing today's soft light. She'd read about the unusual light turquoise green colour of the sea on a warm day, caused by copper in the slate and sand around the area, and here it was spread out right in front of her eyes.

Eventually Tish's stomach rumbled and she put down the pencil to check her watch. Three o'clock and she'd forgotten all about lunch. She flipped through the pages and smiled at the preliminary sketches she'd done for eight ornaments based on the King Arthur legend. It'd take a lot more work before they'd get to the manufacturing stage — but this was the fun part, seeing a vague idea come to life.

Her phone rang and Tish frowned, seeing Sadie's name come up. She wasn't ready for work to intrude just yet, but she was obliged to answer. 'Yeah, how's it going?'

'It's not. Any chance you can come

back early?' Before she could answer, her partner rushed on. 'We've got major problems with the Music City range — they've screwed up the Opry ones and the colour on the Bluebird Café is totally wrong. The samples for Vegas aren't here yet and — '

Tish sighed and ploughed back in. 'Cool it, Sadie. Have them ship the samples straight to our hotel instead and tell Antony to get onto the manufacturer over the colours et cetera. I'll get online as soon as I can and try to change my ticket. I'll call you back later.'

She closed up the phone and cursed under her breath. She hated this side of the business, and the more successful they became the more time she had to spend putting out metaphorical fires instead of designing.

She collected up her things and headed back towards her car. She'd treat herself to one last indulgence and buy a warm pasty on the way back to Boscastle.

A clear picture of her younger self sitting on the beach at Newquay with Nico, one hot summer day when they'd skipped school, stopped her dead in her tracks. The innocence of their teenage love, when they believed nothing and no one could come between them, now seemed as much a fairytale as the King Arthur story.

Tish shook her head and pushed the memories away.

Focus on work. Unlike Nico, it wouldn't let her down. She must accept he was now a part of her past and could never be anything more. Some lessons were hard to swallow and this one stuck hard in her throat.

21

'What on earth are you doing up this early?' Nico rubbed his sleepy eyes and focused on Peter, obviously freshly showered and busy frying bacon at his small kitchen stove.

'Jet lag. Coffee's made. Sit down and I'll serve you, little brother.'

Nico ignored him and stepped across to the coffee pot, pouring himself a much-needed mug of the fragrant, dark liquid. He took a long, deep swallow and a few brain cells began to function. 'Did you sleep well?'

'Like a log, despite the overwhelming smell of paint,' his visitor joked.

'Sorry. I never have guests, it hadn't occurred to me.'

'No matter.' Peter loaded up two plates and dropped one down in front of him. Nico dived in, suddenly starving. They didn't bother talking until they'd worked their way through the tasty pile of bacon, eggs, mushrooms and toast.

Nico pushed his plate away and gulped down the rest of his coffee. 'Thanks. That was good.'

'Are you sure you've eaten any time recently?'

Nico shrugged. 'I didn't bother much yesterday.'

Peter eyed him shrewdly. 'You need a woman around to take care of you. I'd be a mess without Karen.'

With no response, he blithely carried on. 'We don't have much time, so I'm not pussyfooting around. You need to go back to Sicily. Face it. You can't hide out here forever. It's eating you up and you'll never have any sort of life if you don't.'

'What's wrong with my damn life?' Nico retorted, clenching his hands on the edge of the table. 'Last night you told me it was great.'

'In theory it is, but it doesn't take a genius to see you're miserable. I know we don't do the whole talking thing, but you're so tightly wound up I'm surprised you can even breathe. You must be the antithesis of the typical Italian.'

Nico swallowed hard. 'I've had to be. I couldn't survive any other way.' They'd never spoken of this before and he stumbled over his words. 'I saw my family destroyed in front of my eyes, got thrown on the next plane out and sent here to live with people I'd never met. If I'd shown my feelings once, I'd have fallen apart,' he whispered fiercely. 'Plus, I was thirteen, what the hell did you expect?'

His brother flushed and shifted in the chair.

'Sorry. I thought by now . . . didn't they send you to therapy? I remember you disappearing off to Truro and Dad said you had to see someone. I didn't ask any more, I suppose because I was seventeen and didn't want to know too much. I preferred to kick a football around with you or get you interested in girls.'

Peter's wry smile eased something inside Nico.

'It worked. I still love both,' he managed to joke. 'Hate therapists, too. The woman was a pain in the neck. I wasn't about to talk to some droopy old woman who kept talking about giving me 'closure'. I hate that bloody word,' he muttered.

'My uncle rang last week. He calls regularly and tries to get me to go back for a visit.'

'Do you ever seriously consider it, or do you just blast him out of the water?'

Nico hesitated. 'Tish was with me when he phoned. She asked questions and I . . . couldn't answer them.'

'Couldn't or wouldn't?'

'Both. I'm not sure how, plus I was guilty about being with her anyway. All I kept hearing was Dad's voice, asking one thing of me — and I couldn't even keep my promise.'

'It's not necessary any more — so, for

heaven's sake, go after the woman. She'll help you sort the rest out if you give her a chance.' Peter's sudden sympathy made Nico's throat tighten. 'Where is she?'

He shrugged. 'Still up at Beach Road with Annie Treloare, I suppose.'

'Get yourself in the bloody shower, then dress in your fancy clothes so you can put on the smooth Italian act you've got down to a fine art. Go and woo her. Throw yourself on her mercy and admit you've been stupid — women love nothing better.'

A broad smile crept across Nico's face and he leapt to his feet. 'Thanks, mate. I owe you.'

Peter smacked his arm. 'Buy me a pint in the Blue Anchor tonight and we'll reminisce about our under-age drinking days.'

'Deal.' Nico ran from the kitchen and took the narrow stairs two at a time. *Tish Carlisle, I'm coming to get you. We've wasted enough damn time.*

'You're leaving already?' Babs complained. 'But you've only just got here.'

'Work problems. I'm heading straight to Las Vegas because the conference starts in a few days and I can work on the other issues better from there. I know it sounds crazy but the Bluebird Café ornament is bright blue and sparkly instead of faded and worn at the edges. People won't buy if it's not authentic.'

Babs laughed warmly at her. 'Hmmm — no, I certainly wouldn't want my Christmas ornaments all pretty and sparkly.'

'You Cornish people are weird, that's for sure.'

'You're one, too, my dear,' Babs shot right back and a disconcerting shiver ran through Tish's bones. She'd come to think of herself as American . . . until the day she stood outside her old house on Beach Road and realised some things were part of her, whether she wanted them to be or not.

'I'd better go and pack. The sooner I get on the road, the better. I've got a hotel booked near the airport and my flight leaves around eleven tomorrow morning.'

Too fast. She'd wanted to prepare herself to leave, but maybe it was just as well? She wouldn't have any farewells — fond or otherwise — with Nico, that was for sure.

Tish headed upstairs before Babs could delay her with more words of unwanted wisdom.

⋆ ⋆ ⋆

The miles slipped away and Tish was thankful for the years of long-distance driving she'd done in the States which made the four-hour trip seem nothing. With the rental car returned and herself settled in the hotel room, she made a quick call to Annie. It went fine until she asked the one question Tish didn't know how to answer.

'If Nico asks, do I tell him your new plans?'

She should've said a definite no, but at the last second wimped out and said she'd leave it up to Annie's discretion. That drew a wicked chuckle in reply.

Tish struggled to think of something other than Nico's silky brown eyes dragging their gaze down over her skin as his hands explored her needy body. Everything tightened and tingled at the memory of his demanding lovemaking, and how he'd shown her what she'd been missing all these years.

With her hands still shaking, she selected her clothes to wear on the flight. Tomorrow she'd go for elegant and stylish, the way women dressed in the first days of transatlantic travel. A smart powder-blue, fitted suit she'd picked up in a vintage shop in Atlanta, worn with a white blouse, pearls and high-heeled white shoes. At home she had a matching blue pillbox hat, but it would have been squashed in transit so she planned to compromise by doing

her hair in a Jackie Kennedy-style flip
and adding a blue satin headband.

Tish set her alarm and climbed into
the big, empty bed. Sleep wouldn't
come . . . but Nico did, in her dreams,
all night.

★ ★ ★

'When did she leave?' His stomach
roiled as Nico realised he'd left it too
late, again. It was the story of his life.

Annie's inquisitive blue eyes softened
and she beckoned him inside. In the
kitchen she shooed him to sit at the
table and poured them both a cup of
tea.

'Maybe I shouldn't tell you, but she
did say it was up to me if you did ask
— and I think you're both idiots.' He
didn't try to argue with her. 'She went
to stay with my sister in Boscastle to get
away from here, but was needed back at
work so she changed her ticket and is
leaving Heathrow this morning.'

'Back to Nashville?'

'No, she's going straight to Las Vegas for this trade show.'

Nico's brain whirred in fast motion. 'Do you know what hotel she's staying at?'

'No.' Annie's face creased into a slow smile. 'But I'd guess it'd be pretty easy to find out where a Christmas trade show is taking place. You're a smart man.'

No, I'm extremely stupid actually. 'Thanks, Annie — you're a good person.'

'Are you going after her?'

'What do you think?' His ironic tone said it all and she grinned. 'I let her go once because I was too young and foolish. Plus there were . . . complications.' No way could he mention Frank's affair; he'd let her think he meant solely his family's tragic deaths.

'There always are — but we often give them more credence than they deserve.' Her quiet words silenced him for a moment and she held his gaze. For a second he wondered whether she did know about Frank and Elaine, before deciding he really *was* stupid. She'd hardly be sitting here talking pleasantly to him.

'Off you go, and chase after our girl. Bring her back here. It's where she needs to be,' Annie said with certainty.

Nico wished he could be so sure. Yet he had to take the chance, or his life would stay as empty as his heart.

22

Tish glanced around her luxurious room at the Bellagio Las Vegas hotel and thought of Nico for the forty millionth time since they parted. He'd made it clear they had no future so why did he keep turning up in her head — and more importantly why did she persist in letting him back in?

Last night she'd flailed around in the lonely king-sized bed, her body craving him so acutely that she'd woken this morning aching and worn out. A good soak in the massive Italian marble bath tub should have helped, but all she could imagine was what they could do in there together. She'd showered instead.

She could either scream or work, and one option was a lot more sensible than the other. Tish yanked out her sketch pad and made herself open up to the pages with her new designs. Soon the magic worked, and she was engrossed in making detailed sketches of the ornaments from different sides.

As soon as the trade show was over, she'd visit the local Nashville manufacturer she worked with and they'd start on the clay moulds. After they got the details right, they'd move on to the glass version and perfect the hand painting before they considered production.

Tish rubbed at her sore neck and decided to get out of her room. Once Sadie arrived tomorrow they'd be busy, so she'd make the most of her free evening and go outside to see the famous musical fountains before dinner. She should have made time to go home and pick up more clothes, but would have to make do. Las Vegas needed glamour and style, so it would have to be her prized 1950s Chanel dress.

She did a twirl in front of the mirror and smiled at her reflection. The knee-length black taffeta with lace-edged flounces and a wide satin belt was the epitome of femininity and always gave her a boost. She picked up the small beaded clutch bag she'd tracked down online and never yet used.

You'll do. He doesn't know what he's missing.

For a second her vision filled with a clear picture of Nico, his eyes burning with passion and staring at her with such longing that a deep-seated ache tugged at her gut.

You are not going to stay in here and mope for another minute. Get out. Now.

She swung around on her heels and stalked out of the room, slamming the door behind her.

★ ★ ★

Nico sat on the edge of the bed, frozen in place. He tried to blame jet-lag but it was a feeble excuse. Tish was somewhere in this massive, opulent hotel

— beautiful, intelligent, funny and no doubt still mad as hell at him.

Whatever had he been thinking of, coming here?

Get yourself in the bloody shower, then dress in your fancy clothes so you can put on the smooth Italian act you've got down to a fine art. Go and woo her. Throw yourself on her mercy and admit you've been stupid — women love nothing better.

Peter's words echoed in his head. They were as good a road map as anything he could come up with. Nico dragged himself to his feet and unzipped his garment bag. He hung up the new Italian linen suit he'd picked up from the Armani spring collection and selected a soft-collared white shirt to wear open-necked.

Stripping off his travel clothes, he headed for the bathroom and stepped into the glass-enclosed shower, allowing the shards of steaming hot water to pound his tired muscles. When he couldn't take any more, he stepped out and pulled on one of the thick, white robes, grabbing a towel from the heated rail to rub his wet hair. He wandered over to the panoramic window, pressed the control to open the curtains and watched the lighted fountains playing thirty floors down. He'd get dressed and leave a message for Tish at the reception desk. After that, it'd be a question of waiting. He'd have a wander around and — just maybe — Lady Luck would smile on him for once.

★ ★ ★

She did.

Music hummed in the sultry air while the fountains played their choreographed dance, to the fascination of the large crowd gathered in front of the hotel. Nico's attention zoomed straight in on her. In the middle of a sea of ordinary people Tish's striking beauty reached out and grabbed him by the throat.

He pushed his way through, not caring about the muttered complaints. Almost within reach of Tish, a staggering drunk bumped into her and he saw her struggle to keep her balance.

Pushing closer, he grabbed the man roughly by the collar, shoving him to one side. 'Go and annoy someone else,' he growled.

'Nico!' Her startled expression wasn't one of undiluted joy, but then he hadn't expected it to be. 'What on earth are you doing here?'

The white lights, flashing in time to the music, illuminated her beautiful face and he wanted to seize hold of her and plant a kiss on her glossy, red lips. Of course he'd receive a hard slap for such foolishness.

'What do you think?'

She pulled back her shoulders and glared. 'I don't know, which is why I asked.'

The music built towards its thrilling climax and gave him a stupid courage. Nico planted his hands on her slim waist, his fingers stroking the black silk of her stunning dress, its sleeveless top and tiered skirt emphasising her luscious curves.

'Let's go somewhere quiet.'

She tilted her chin and threw him a defiant stare.

'I came to watch the fountains and I'm going to stay until the end. You can do what you like.' Tonight her eyes were a deep shade of jade and their beauty pulled him closer.

'We'll watch together and then we'll talk,' he said quietly. She didn't argue and he turned her back to face the fountains, replaced his hands and leaned slightly against her back to remind her he was there.

The crowd gasped as the jets of water soared towards the night sky and Nico's senses expanded with the music; the roar of the fountains, the erotic touch of Tish under his fingers and the scent of her body, sending him close to madness.

'Wasn't that the most wonderful

thing you've ever seen?' A wonderful smile lit up her face and she shone with undiluted pleasure.

'I can see the fountains from my suite. It's on the thirtieth floor,' he said hopefully.

'You must be mad. After the way you treated me, you think I'm rushing off to your bedroom because I've been captivated by a few fountains? I'll allow you to buy me dinner because I'm famished, and I'll listen to what pathetic excuse you've come up with for your appalling behaviour, but don't expect miracles,' she snapped.

Nico nodded — he'd have been disappointed if she'd succumbed too easily. He deserved to work for forgiveness.

'I have a table booked at the Picasso outdoor patio if it suits you?'

'How did you manage that? I've heard people make reservations there months in advance.' Her eyes narrowed.

A breath hitched in Nico's throat and

he decided it was time for the first truth.

'Jake Worthington who oversees the Bellagio's art collection is a friend of mine. He purchased the Picassos for the restaurant.' He dared to pick up her hands and she didn't pull away. 'You asked me once if I'd given up my dream of being a famous artist, and I lied because I've got used to keeping it secret. I never stopped painting, and I've achieved a certain level of success. They held an exhibition of my work here a couple of years ago.'

'You're kidding me — aren't you?' Nico heard her uncertainty and didn't blame her.

'No. Have you heard of Enigma?' Her mouth shaped a wide O and he almost laughed. 'I'll take that as a yes.'

'But why?' Her elegant hands waved in a gesture of confusion. 'Why don't you put your own name on them? They're wonderful. I've lusted over them for years but I keep putting all my money back in the business. I've promised myself I'll buy one when I retire.'

Nico saw the half-finished portrait of Tish in his head and grinned. 'You shall have one, I promise. As for the name — I'm . . . very private, as you know, and I didn't want the publicity.'

He reached up to rest his hand on the soft curve of her cheek. 'Let's go and eat. The food is wonderful and we can take our time walking through the restaurant. You'll enjoy the atmosphere they've created.'

For the first time since he'd surprised her with his arrival, Tish succumbed to a tight smile. 'It explains one of the puzzling things about you. I wondered how an underpaid Cornish solicitor could afford to dress like an Armani model, but now I know.'

A rush of heat flamed Nico's skin. 'Don't exaggerate.'

'I'm not. You've really no idea, do you? With your looks and style, you stand out no matter how much you think you're blending in.' She smirked.

'I love it, by the way, because I adore anything or anybody creative whether it's clothes, art or music. Even as a teenager you were different to the local boys. The combination of that and your cute accent made you irresistible.'

'Irresistible? You've done a pretty good job of resisting recently,' he observed with a wry smile. 'Come on.'

Nico tucked her hand through his arm and steered them back towards the hotel. Maybe this crazy idea of his would work.

He'd never seen anyone's jaw drop literally, but Tish's did and she exhaled a low, happy sigh as she spotted the first Picasso on entering the restaurant.

'It's incredible. He was such a genius. Look at the depth of colour . . . ' She blushed and he'd never seen anything so lovely.

'This is my favourite.' He led her over to the stunning masterpiece on the way into the dining room and for a few minutes they both stood absolutely still and studied it greedily. To share this level of appreciation with her was special. Helena's interest in art was cultivated to impress other people, but Tish's was as deep-rooted as his own.

'I can see why,' she murmured and squeezed his hand, her heated touch sending a rush of blood to places he struggled to keep under control.

'Do you want to look at the ceramics collection now, or after we eat?' he asked, the voice tight in his throat, and she smiled coyly up at him.

'After. I'll have them for dessert.'

Nico caught the maître d's eye and indicated they were ready. He'd pulled every string to get the table favoured with the prime view of the fountains. Tish bounced along next to him as they made their way around to the edge of the patio, everything about her glowing with the pleasure of the moment. He hoped she would still be smiling when he told her the rest of his story.

They placed their order and the waiter poured the Californian wine Nico had selected with their first course, a Maine lobster salad they'd both chosen.

He raised his glass in a toast. 'To Picasso.'

She took a sip of wine and smiled in approval before placing the cut-crystal glass back on the table. A look of determination crossed her face and she placed her hand on his, the warmth of her soft, fragrant skin tugging at his heart.

'It's time, Nico. I meant what I said when I left you in Cornwall and it'll take a hell of a lot on your part to change my mind.'

Nico nodded and took a fortifying swallow of wine, wishing it had the kick of his favorite grappa, and began.

23

Tish took several deep breaths, still unable to believe he'd tracked her down across the Atlantic after the way they parted. She wished he wasn't so handsome tonight, the flickering lights gleaming on his thick brown hair as it grazed the collar of his immaculate white shirt. A shadow of late-day stubble highlighted his firm jaw, making her fingers itch to run over his tanned skin. Nico's eyes fixed on her, dark as night and equally sinful.

Mentally she slapped herself. *Remember how he treated you.*

'You asked about my family.' His facial muscles tightened and the air around them vibrated with tension. For a second she almost told him it didn't matter but kept silent, hating to cause him pain but needing to hear it from his own lips.

He gulped down his wine and glanced down at the table, fiddling with hem of the blue linen napkin. 'My father was a lawyer, too — he was a prosecutor in Sicily and a sworn enemy of organised crime and drug-running. He hated what it was doing to his people. He escaped two assassination attempts and was in the middle of a high profile case which would put several top people behind bars for life if he was successful.'

The waiter arrived with their salads. Awkwardly Tish thanked him as Nico stared grimly at the plate of food.

'We always had Sunday dinner at my Nonna's house and everyone was ready to go except me.' He sucked in an audible breath. 'My mother insisted I kept on my church clothes and wouldn't let me change into jeans, so I refused to go.'

'Teenagers are naturally rebellious. I was terrible to my mother too, especially after we moved.'

Nico stared blankly in her direction

and Tish knew he didn't see her.

'My father was furious, I'd never heard him so angry. He told me to stay at home and ordered our cook not to let me have anything to eat. They were late leaving because of me. Usually he let his security man check the car before going anywhere but he waved him away, saying he didn't have time. We'd used it for church an hour before, so he assumed it'd be fine.'

'That sounds reasonable.'

Nico scowled and knocked back the rest of his wine, quickly refilling his glass and drinking half of that in one gulp. 'I stood at our front door, arrogant as hell, and shouted at my father as he unlocked the car. I called him a jerk and said I wouldn't be there when he got home. My mother and sister got into the car . . . ' His voice faded and he went deathly pale.

'Your sister? I never knew you had a sister.'

His eyes turned glassy with unshed tears. 'Caterina was eight and so beautiful, and she adored me. She cried and pleaded with me to come but I told her not to be a silly little girl.'

'Nico, what happened?' Tish whispered, afraid of what must be coming next.

'My father started the car and . . . it blew up. A loud, raging fireball right in front of my eyes. Two of my father's staff held me back.' He swallowed hard. 'I tried to get to them but they wouldn't let me.' His shoulders heaved with suppressed emotion and Tish reached out to cradle his hands in her own, desperate to give him some measure of comfort.

'There was nothing you could've done, my love, you'd have died too.'

He raised his eyes back to her and sighed, so deeply it slashed through her heart.

'Do you think I'd have cared? They were everything to me. I should have been with them.'

She'd never felt so helpless, searching for something to say which wasn't trite and meaningless.

'In your heart you know they loved you too and would rejoice that you survived. They'd want you to live a happy, productive life and remember them all in a good way.'

Nico pulled away from her, finishing his wine and slamming the glass back on the table. 'Don't you think I've heard all those useless platitudes before? They've been spouted at me by everyone — therapists, the Penwarrens and what's left of my family — it makes no damn difference. I've still got this gaping hole inside which nothing fills.' He spread his large, trembling hands on the white tablecloth and went very still. 'For a while I thought our love might be enough and you'd make me whole again, but it was a foolish dream.'

His bitter words scared her, but suddenly a clear sensation of rightness ran through her body.

'If you ask me, we haven't given it a real chance,' she murmured, fixing him with a calm smile.

'Sir, madam. Would you care for me to clear away your salads?' The waiter's question took them both by surprise and Tish saw she needed to answer for both of them as Nico was staring at her, stunned.

'Yes, please. We aren't very hungry. It was delicious — but could you bring the check, please?'

The waiter cleared their plates and left. She turned back calmly to Nico.

'How about we find somewhere quiet where we can talk over a cup of coffee?'

* * *

Nico chose the seat across from her in the dark corner of the small café and waited for her to speak first. He drank in the sight of her, always an intoxicating mixture of elegant and sweet, and longed to touch her again.

'Who were you speaking to in Italian the other night?'

'My Zio, my uncle, Antonio — he's my mother's brother and takes care of our house on Mount Etna. He routinely rings and tries to persuade me to visit. For years he plied the same line as everyone else — that it would free me emotionally — but now he's trying a different angle, saying it's my responsibility to care for my inheritance.' Nico managed a wry smile. 'He's right, of course.'

'They might all be right,' she murmured, the soft Southern drawl she'd picked up seducing him all over again. 'You won't ever be happy without laying this to rest. Naturally you'll always miss your family, but if you can lay down this crippling burden of guilt you're hauling around, wouldn't it be freeing?'

'I don't know how to,' he said simply and her face softened into such heartbreaking sympathy that he barely held himself together.

'Would you try if I helped you?'

'You'd be willing to do that after the way I've treated you?' he asked, although her glistening eyes gave him the answer. 'Why, Tish?'

'Why do you think, you idiot? Because I love you and always have.' Tish's shy smile unmanned him. 'God knows why, because you're the most stubborn, exasperating man I've ever met. The trouble is, no one else ever came close to my memory of you and, since we've made love, I can't imagine ever being with any other man.'

A delicate blush rose up her elegant neck and coloured her porcelain skin. He leaned across the table to trail a lingering finger down the side of her face and smiled as she leaned into him, a soft moan of pleasure escaping her.

'I can't bear to think of any other man touching you either.' He rasped out the words. 'I've always loved you too, but . . . there's more you need to know.'

Her eyes sparkled and she pressed a soft kiss on his forehead. 'Later. You've said all I need to hear for tonight. Do you know what I want to do with you now?' Her tongue licked teasingly over

269

her glossy lips and Nico's groin tightened.

'You're killing me, baby, you know that, right?' His growl sent a mischievous smile zipping across her face. The letters could wait for another day; he couldn't.

'Your room or mine?'

'Mine's bigger,' Nico murmured suggestively, and watched her blush again.

'It would be. Yours it is then.'

They stood at the same moment and he slid his hand down to rest at the base of her spine, caressing her backside through the stiff fabric of her dress. 'The lift is over there.'

'Good, so is the elevator,' she teased and he grabbed her, pulling her to him and seizing her mouth in a deep, plundering kiss, unable to wait another second.

He pulled away before he could embarrass them both and steered her across the room, his heart thumping in his chest. As the lift doors opened, the two other couples already in there shifted to give them space.

Nico eased her up against the mirrored wall and bent down to whisper in her ear. 'You know what I'd do now if we were alone, don't you?'

She cradled his face and pretended to kiss him back while murmuring against his heated skin.

'I'd let you, too, and love it.' She slid her hand down between them and lightly trailed her fingers over his growing arousal.

'Witch.' A raw ache lodged deep inside him and Nico pushed her hand away and shook his head. 'Take pity on me.'

'Why? You never have done on me.' Tish's wicked laugh drove him crazy.

One couple got out and Nico shifted himself in front of her, pushing her further back into the corner. 'Five floors to go, can you wait that long?' He teased a finger down her throat to rest on the curve of her breast, her heart racing beneath his touch.

271

The other couple left at the next floor and with only seconds left before they reached the thirtieth floor, Nico insinuated his hand under her dress and smiled as he reached her thigh and touched bare, smooth skin.

'Stockings. Did you know I was coming?'

A teasing grin spread across her face. 'I sure hope you're going to wait at least a few more minutes.'

The lift door opened and Nico dragged her out into the hallway. 'This way.'

At his suite door he fumbled in his pocket for the key card, suddenly having ten thumbs, none of which worked. Then he pushed open the door and yanked her inside, kicking it shut.

'Wow. I thought I had a nice room but this is something else.'

'Tish, forget the damn room.' He grasped hold of her bare shoulders and stared into her eyes. 'If you don't want your beautiful dress ruined, get it off now.'

She threw him a mock glare. 'You ruin this and you're a dead man.' Slowly she turned around and glanced back provocatively over her shoulder. 'Carefully unzip me, and I mean carefully, so I can step out of it. When I've laid it somewhere safe out of your reach, then I'm all yours.'

Nico couldn't speak. He ordered his trembling fingers to follow her instructions and somehow did what she asked. She stepped onto the plush, pale blue carpet in her bra, thong and stockings, giving a little wiggle as she crossed to a chair and draped the dress over it. Then, at last, she beckoned him to her.

Two rapid strides and he stood in front of her. Nico let his gaze travel down over her glorious body, her skin flushing a delicate shade of pink as he lingered on her black lace bra, down over her stomach to the black thong. Her breathing quickened and he slid one hand downwards, stroking tenderly through the lace and satin and making her pulse against him.

'You want me, don't you?' Her damp neediness made him throb with the overwhelming urge to bury himself inside her.

Nico tore his hands away and stripped in a matter of seconds, tossing his clothes carelessly around the floor. 'Later we'll take our time, but right now I'm out of patience.'

'Yes, sir.' Jokingly she saluted and gasped as he scooped her into his arms and flung her on the bed, hastily pulling back the covers and scattering pillows everywhere.

Nico's hands shook as he found the protection he'd brought, just in case, and readied himself. He eased between her thighs, pushing them open wider with his legs and stared down, burning the image of her into his brain. Eyes wide open, her skin flushed and trembling, her hands reaching for him. He'd never forget this until there was no life left in his body.

'Look at me. I want to watch when I make you come.'

Very slowly he pushed into her, loving her groan as he filled her completely. He held still until she writhed under him, her hips undulating and urging him deeper. Nico pulled back and thrust hard. She gasped but he never stopped, pounding into her as she wrapped her legs around his waist, matching him breath for breath.

'Come on, sweetheart, come with me.' His finger rested on her sweet spot and her face burst into a radiance, sending him crashing over the edge as they reached the peak together. His release went on and on while her body continued to pulse around him, gradually slowing to a teasing shiver against his searing hot skin.

Nico collapsed onto her, vaguely aware after a few seconds that his weight must be crushing her.

'I'll have to move.' He pushed himself up on his elbows and eased from her body, hating her sigh of disappointment. He lay beside her, wrapping himself around her skin to skin, and nuzzled against her neck.

'Sleep, baby, sleep.' He stroked her silky, black hair and watched her eyes droop with contented tiredness.

She might turn on him tomorrow when she saw the letters, but he'd savour tonight for the miracle it was and worry about the next problem in the morning. He clung onto her earlier loving words, desperate to believe that they could make a go of this.

24

The cheerful melody of her ringtone jerked Tish awake, but she found she couldn't move. She was pinned to the bed, entangled tightly with Nico's large, hot, naked body. Wonderful — but she needed to find her phone.

'Shift, my handsome hunk.' She pushed at him and he groaned, pulling her tighter. 'Nico. I've got to answer it.'

He stirred enough for her to wriggle out of the bed. Stumbling around in the dark, she tracked down her handbag. Of course the second she located her cell phone it stopped ringing, so she checked her missed calls and found Sadie's name.

'Come back here.' Nico pulled at her arm and she met his dark chocolate gaze. How was she supposed to think of work with him rubbing up against her skin, setting everything tingling all over again?

'I'm sorry, I've got to call Sadie back. Remember I'm here to work. No fun, I know, but it's my life.'

His face shadowed and she wished the last words unsaid. Turning away, she punched in the number and waited.

'Where are you? I've been calling your room for the last hour.'

Tish blushed, very glad they didn't have videophones. 'I was up early and . . . went down for breakfast. How about I come to your room in about thirty minutes and we'll get started?'

She met Nico's amused grin as she closed up the phone.

'Have a good breakfast, did you?'

Tish leapt from the bed, evading his outstretched arm. 'Stop it, you monster. I've got to go and shower before I meet Sadie or she'll guess what I've been up to.' He checked her out very obviously as she hastily pulled on her dress, not bothering with underwear. That she stowed in her bag and pulled her shoes back on, without stockings. She ached to rip it all off and jump back in bed with him again but forced herself to resist.

'I've no idea what time I can come back. I've tons to do.'

His handsome face softened into a sexy smile and her willpower wobbled like an unset jelly.

'Don't apologise. It's your business and I did drop in unexpectedly. You've got my mobile number, so just call or text if you have a minute. I'm fascinated by the casinos and want to do some sketches for a possible painting.'

She knelt back on the bed and cupped his face in her hands. 'I know we need to talk more, but this isn't a good time for me. We'll be through by Friday and then I'm free for the weekend.'

She couldn't afford to be distracted, and he did that to her every time. Every cell in her body was on high alert as he watched her leave the room, but he didn't try to stop her and she was grateful. Focusing on work for the rest of the day would help with everything else.

Being in love wasn't a normal state of mind for her and it took some getting used to. She'd put work first for so long that she'd forgotten how to have a normal life.

★　★　★

Her clothes stuck to her sweaty body as Tish pinned up the last poster and adjusted the arrangement of the ornaments for about the fiftieth time.

'Well, that'll have to do,' she declared to Sadie.

'It looks great. Can you believe it's eight o'clock? Where's the day gone?' Sadie shoved a hand through her thick, blonde hair and laughed. 'Now we get to sample the nightlife. Are you up to a twirl around the casino? We can put our fancy frocks on and see if Prince Charming is waiting for us.'

Tish didn't know how to answer, she'd tried several times to tell her friend and partner about Nico but the words never came out. 'I can't, really . . . well, I could, but . . . '

'What's up? You've been twitchy all day. At first I put it down to nerves about the show, but you've checked your phone about a million times and every time the ballroom door opened you jerked around like someone shot you.'

Tish felt like a teenager confessing to her first crush.

'In Cornwall I sort of met up again with a Sicilian I knew years ago and we've gotten involved. He's here staying and I'm not sure what his plans are tonight.' Her voice faded away and she couldn't quite meet her friend's curiosity.

'You are a sly one. Are you tellin' me he came all this way to see you?'

Tish shrugged. 'Well . . . yeah.'

'Is he cute?' Sadie probed, a big grin on her face.

'Answer the lady, sweetheart.' Tish shrieked as Nico's rumbling voice boomed right by her ear. He pressed a light kiss on her cheek, sending a wave of musky cologne her way and putting her body on instant alert. If it was possible, he looked even more handsome tonight in close-fitting black jeans and an open-necked dark red shirt, the sleeves rolled up to show off his muscular arms.

'You don't need to, Tish, hon, I can see for myself.' Sadie admired Nico openly and he returned her stare with a smile.

'I came to see how you're doing. I've got a table booked for a late supper for the three of us in an hour, if you'll be through by then.'

'I won't intrude — '

Nico interrupted before Sadie could finish. 'I'm the intruder and if you still have work to discuss, I'll leave you alone.' He slid an arm around Tish's waist and she leaned into him blissfully before quickly pulling away.

'I must smell terrible! We've been at it all day. We're filthy.'

His warm smile unfurled a rush of desire and she wanted him so badly that it hurt.

'Show me what you've done, and then I'll let you both go and clean up.' He kissed her neck. 'Not that I've any complaints, you always smell wonderful to me.' His stage whisper made Tish heat up to boiling point.

'Here it is.' She waved a hand towards their display and launched into details of what they were showcasing in a bid to win orders for this Christmas and beyond from retailers all over the world. Finally she ran out of steam. She caught Nico's thoughtful gaze lingering on her.

'Very impressive.'

'Thanks.' Suddenly she felt shy, and turned to face Sadie again. 'How about we meet down in the lobby under the Chihuly chandelier a little before nine?'

'Sounds good to me, I'll see you there.' Sadie smiled brightly and headed for the door.

Nico rubbed Tish's back, instantly easing some of the knotted tension in her spine. 'Can I come and watch you dress? I've missed you all day.' His eyes burned into her and she could only nod. He disarmed her every time.

★　★　★

'You're being very thoughtful. I was sure you'd pounce on me as soon as we were alone.' Tish tilted her head and gave him a puzzled look.

'Sweetheart, I'd happily seduce you right now, but for a start we've got a dinner date, and for another thing you're obviously exhausted,' he said lightly. 'As you said, it's not the time for more serious talk, so why don't we save all that for Friday?'

'Will you show me the work you've done later?' she asked. 'I'm baffled how you've managed to hide your identity for so long. I've searched for Enigma on the net and there's nothing out there on you, apart from wild speculation.'

Nico smirked, he couldn't help it. 'My agent knows he won't get his obscenely large percentage if he breaks our agreement. When it's possible he arranges a private viewing of my exhibition so I can see it staged, but otherwise I never attend them. I don't do any publicity; I leave it completely up to him. You know I live a very private life.'

Tish frowned and started to undo the buttons on her blue shirt. The sight stirred his blood, making him ache to take her again, and to hell with eating.

'Didn't Helena ever guess?' she asked.

'No.' How did he explain their odd relationship to someone who was so open in everything she did? 'We only met up a couple of times a week. I paint in my spare bedroom and she's never been upstairs in my house. Before you ask, I never . . . made love to her there, we always went to her place.'

Tish stopped in the middle of

wriggling out of her jeans. 'There's an awful lot I don't know about you, isn't there?'

'I don't want to hide anything from you any more,' Nico said truthfully. 'I've never sought that with anyone else. I hope it's not a burden?'

Please say no. He held his breath as a sly smile tugged at the corners of her lush mouth.

'It's an honour.'

Her soft, smooth drawl entranced him and Nico pulled her to him, teasing her lips with his tongue until she let him in, responding with her own explorations. A few minutes later, he pushed himself forcibly away. 'Get in the shower before I lose the few atoms of commonsense you've left me with. We'll never make dinner otherwise.'

Tish pouted so charmingly he had to laugh.

'Don't worry, you're not the only one suffering.' He placed her hand on his groin, groaning as she caressed him through his jeans, rubbing the rough fabric against his taut, hot skin.

'Sadie wants to check out the casino afterwards.' She took pity and let go of him. Nico breathed again.

'I'll be my most charming and make polite conversation while we eat, but don't expect me to wait any longer than absolutely necessary to get you back in my bed again afterwards.'

'But — '

'I've had a genius idea. You pretty yourself up, and I'll find your friend a much better alternative to frustrating us all evening.'

Tish tried to protest but he silenced her with a swift, hard kiss. 'She'll love it, trust me.'

For once she smiled and didn't argue. He'd chalk that up.

★   ★   ★

Tish clutched Nico's hand and gawked up at the ceiling. No words could describe her reaction to the famous Chihuly chandelier.

'I've seen pictures of this before, but they don't compare to seeing it live.'

'He's a genius.'

'Two thousand hand-blown glass blossoms. Can you imagine the time it must've taken? The colours are amazing. There was an exhibition of his work at the Cheekwood Gardens in Nashville last year, and I went every single day I could escape from work. My favourite time to go was at night when they were illuminated. They appeared to live and breathe, if that doesn't sound crazy.'

Nico shrugged. 'Hey, you're talking to a man who paints mysterious, dark pictures even he doesn't completely understand. I know crazy.'

She took his hands and fixed her bewitching eyes on him. Nico's heart raced, guessing she was close to saying something important.

'There you are! I thought I'd miss you in all these people.' Sadie gave a raucous laugh and reluctantly Nico pulled his gaze away from Tish.

'Ladies, I've something special lined up. We're eating in the Picasso room and my friend Jake Worthington, the curator, is joining us. After supper he'll give us a private tour of the collection.' He glowed at Tish's satisfied nod, and Sadie lit up brighter than a Christmas tree.

'You've got a keeper in this one,' Sadie joked and Nico fought to stop the rush of heat to his skin, getting a kick out of Tish's matching blush.

He ushered Sadie in first and managed to whisper in Tish's ear as they walked along. 'Jake's got his instructions to charm your friend and offer to take her to the casino later.'

'What did you have to promise him?' she teased.

'Apart from my firstborn child? Just for him to have my next exhibition over here,' Nico retorted.

'Am I worth it?'

'Absolutely.' He grabbed her hand and forced her to look up at him. 'Never ask that again.'

He'd planned to wait until Friday, but he would ask her an important question tonight and keep his fingers crossed that he wouldn't lose his nerve if she said yes.

25

Skin against skin, they lay wrapped around each other in his bed and Nico nuzzled into the curve of Tish's neck, smelling her wonderful scent — an arousing mixture of roses, heat and satisfied woman. Twice had barely taken the edge off his desire. He should leave her alone because she needed to sleep, but he couldn't resist. He groped to find another foil packet on the bedside table.

'Again? You're insatiable.' Her low, sexy laugh turned him on even more and he shifted to nestle his growing erection against her. Tish opened to him with a languid sigh.

'It'll be slow and gentle, I promise.' He dropped kisses all the way down her face, then captured her mouth as 'he entered her with a level of control he'd never achieved before. As he sank all the way in, she moved her hips in rhythm with him. It resembled a sinuous dance where both partners knew their moves and were in perfect synch with each other. Nico grasped her hips, stilling her enough to slow things down even more, and she writhed under him.

'Please. I need you now. Don't make me wait,' she panted, a film of sweat beading on her porcelain skin.

'What do you need, my love?' he crooned into her skin, moving to take one breast into his mouth and sucking hard.

'You. Hard. Now.' She tried to thrust up onto him and the fiery demands of her body shook his attempt at control.

'Are you sure?' Nico rasped, seizing a handful of her silky hair and twisting it in his hand to make her meet his gaze.

'Yes!' she exhaled on a long sigh and he broke.

'You asked for it, baby.' Slowly he pulled nearly all the way out and then reared back and slammed into her, hearing her cry out, but way beyond being careful. He plundered her body with his own and she met him with everything she possessed.

'Oh, Nico.' Her body tightened around him and he yelled out her name, giving in to his own pleasure.

Several minutes later, the last aftershocks of their loving ended and he wrapped her in his arms, unable to leave her body.

'Did I hurt you?' he murmured and she gave him the most wondrous smile.

'You gave me exactly what I asked for. I love you, Nico. I've always loved you.'

He stroked her cheek and kissed her lips, pink and swollen from his loving. 'I love you too, more than I'll ever be able to express.' Nico eased out of her and rolled back onto the sheets, unsure how to begin.

'What is it, sweetheart?' Her fingers tangled in his hair and he sighed. She knew him so well — but then she always had done. Even at the tender age of eleven, she'd partially seen through the hard front he'd put on to cover up his pain.

'I know you're busy with work, but I have to ask if you'll do something with me.'

She gave a deliciously sly grin. 'You mean other than what we've just done?'

'Well, that too, I hope, but — ' He stumbled over the words, losing his earlier certainty.

'Have you finally decided to take everyone's advice and go back to Sicily?'

Nico stared at her in shock, and nodded.

Instantly she took his face in her hands, rubbing her fingers over his deliciously stubbled jaw. 'I'd be privileged. When do you want to go?'

This part he hadn't prepared, not daring to think any further than actually asking the question.

'Whatever suits you,' he mumbled, sounding like an inarticulate oaf.

'Well, I've got to wrap up some

things here and I couldn't be gone for long, but let's say in a couple of weeks.'

'Are you sure?'

She silenced him with a finger on his mouth. 'Yes, I'm sure. If I wasn't, I'd say so — you should know me well enough by now to know that.'

Tish glanced up from under her long lashes and nibbled at her lip. 'I know you said we'd wait until the weekend but I need to know now. What else were you going to tell me? We can't have any more secrets, Nico. We've surely gone beyond that.'

She was right, but he hated to spoil a wonderful evening, and surely it would. Suddenly he was saved by her irritating, cheerful mobile ringtone. He tried to hide his relief as she reached for her phone on the bedside table.

'Yeah, what's up, Sadie?' Tish shoved a hand through her hair in exasperation. 'You're kidding me.' She listened some more, muttering and sighing. 'Ok, ok. I'll get on to it right away. You told them I'd call after seven their time?'

She glanced at the glowing digital clock and groaned. 'Thanks, I'll let you know what they say.'

Tish slammed the phone shut and gave Nico an apologetic shrug. 'Sorry, I've got to go to my room and call Paris.'

'Do it from here,' Nico pleaded, not wanting to let her go.

'I can't. All my files and information are there.' She grinned at him. 'Plus I don't need the distraction of you sprawled naked on the bed leering at me.'

'I do not leer and I can cover up,' he teased but grabbed her hand, turning serious. 'It's ok, I understand. Off you go.'

She slid from the bed and started pulling on her clothes. 'You know, I hate this part of my job and every time it happens, I get this much closer to chucking it all in. I love designing, but I never expected a small ornament business in my mother's spare bedroom to turn into this.'

Nico chose his next words carefully, not wanting to put any pressure on her. 'It's a big decision. Maybe when you get away to Sicily with me, it'll give you a chance to think more clearly.'

Her warm smile sent pleasant shivers all through him.

'You're a good man, Nico, and a good lawyer too. I appreciate you not trying to sway me — though there'll come a point when I want your opinion.' She threatened him with a wag of her finger.

'And when you do, I'll give it to you,' he said quietly and grinned. 'Of course, you know I charge by the hour.'

She leaned back down to the bed and trailed a finger down from his chest along the thin line of dark hair headed south, stirring him to life again. 'Oh, I think you might give me a freebie if I'm a good girl.'

He growled at her torturing touch. 'You're never good — which is why I love you. And if you don't go right now, I'll have you flat on your back being really bad again.'

Tish leaped away and flashed him a wicked smile. 'I'm off to work and I'll see you tomorrow, Mr De Burgh.' She ran from the room, turning at the door to give him a long, lascivious wink.

Nico rolled back on the bed and groaned.

★　★　★

Tish wrapped up the conversation and tossed the phone back on the bed. Another manufacturing glitch sorted, and a major customer happy again. All she felt was weary; looking at the clock, she realised it was three o'clock in the morning. She wandered over to the window and pressed the control switch to open the drapes. Las Vegas in all its glittering, overblown glory was spread out in front of her, but its attractions didn't tempt her in the least. The only thing on her mind was the man she'd left.

Going with him to Sicily was a huge

step for them both, and it could either strengthen or quench what they'd reignited. Tonight she'd almost confessed she knew what he wanted to talk about, but had held her tongue. Making him tell her would prove that he had no more secrets.

She yawned and walked back over to flop on the bed. For two pins she'd creep upstairs to Nico, but then she really wouldn't get any sleep. As her head hit the pillow, her last thoughts were how great it would be to sneak these luxurious bed linens home with her . . . and of a certain Sicilian whom she intended to make her own.

★　★　★

'Here, drink this and sit down for a minute, girl.' Sadie thrust a can of soda at Tish and pushed her down onto one of the chairs behind their display. 'The crowd's thinning out now — they're all thinking of finding dinner and hitting the casinos.'

'Thanks.' Tish popped open the top and took a long, deep swallow, waiting for the surge of energy she badly needed to get through the next hour until the show closed. She glanced around her. 'We've done great today.'

'Yeah, we have — so why don't you have a broad smile at the thought of all the orders and the money we're going to make?'

Tish shrugged and couldn't quite meet her partner's eyes.

'Is all this to do with the lusty Sicilian waiting in his penthouse suite to do unmentionable things to you yet again?' she teased. 'Don't worry, I'm just envious. I think I'm all dried up, it's been so long.'

Sadie's wry laugh broke through Tish's reserve and she smiled back.

'What about Jake Worthington? He's sexy and seemed pretty interested in you last night.'

A tinge of colour highlighted Sadie's cheeks and Tish knew she'd hit the bull's eye.

'He did offer to show me his private art collection tonight.'

Tish chuckled. 'I'll bet he did. Do you think he's got any masterpieces?' They cracked up into infectious giggles.

'Oh, I think he might, and I'm considering taking him up on the offer.' Sadie stared hard at Tish. 'Don't change the subject. What about the famous Nico? What's goin' on between you two? Will I be looking for a new business partner soon?'

Put on the spot, Tish was speechless. She took another drink and tried to decide how best to answer.

'You know I've been restless for a while. I hate all this.' She waved her arm around the room. 'You're in your element, but I have to make myself do it.'

'Don't do anything rash.' Sadie's vehemence startled Tish. 'We've put a hell of lot of work into getting where we are.'

'I know. Nico said the same.'

'You've spoken to him about it

already?' Sadie sounded hurt, but Tish needed to be honest.

'Briefly, last night. We'll be able to talk more now the show is finished. I might be going to Sicily with him in a couple of weeks — I'm not sure yet.'

'Are you mad? With Christmas in only four months? We're snowed under,' Sadie protested.

Tish put down her drink. 'It's not up for discussion. I understand it's a bad time but I need to do this for Nico because there are things he needs to face from his past, and for myself because I need to take a step back and focus on my life outside work. Also it's for us together — I hope we'll find out where this is going. I'm sorry to drop you in it, Sadie, but I've no choice.'

She realised the truth of the words as she said them and found it freeing.

Sadie shrugged. 'Ok. I'll carry things while you're gone — but afterwards we'll have to sort things out properly. Get someone else in if necessary.'

Tish reached for Sadie's hand.

'Thanks. I promise I'll know by then. You've been a rock. Now why don't you leave me to finish off here while you run off and put on the sexy red dress I saw hanging in your room and go check out Mr Worthington's collection?'

The bright smile returned to her partner's face. 'I won't argue. I've arranged for everything to be picked up in the morning and shipped back to Nashville, so I guess I'll see you back at work on Monday.'

'Definitely.' Tish crossed her fingers, wondering if she was over-optimistic about the future with Nico. She wanted to believe they'd been given a second chance for a good reason.

26

Nico grasped a tight hold of the phone to stop from shaking. 'Si, zia, Aunt Maria, I understand.' He sucked in a deep breath and quietly gave the only answer possible. 'I'll be there as soon as I can. I can't get a flight out now until the morning and it'll be Tuesday before I'll be with you. I might have someone with me. I don't know yet.'

Nico smiled at his aunt's pointed questions. 'You'll have to wait and see. Give my love to Uncle Antonio . . .' His throat tightened. 'Tell him to be strong.'

He hung up and dropped down onto the bed. Life was so unfair. If his uncle died before he arrived, he could add something else to his list of unforgivable actions. He'd made a rational decision to return to Sicily, and now was being thrust back before he was prepared — although in truth he'd never be ready even if he waited another nineteen years.

'Who was on the phone?' Tish, her skin pink and glowing and with only a towel wrapped around her, appeared in the bathroom doorway. 'I'd hoped to have company in your amazing tub.' She pouted and he managed to smile.

But she knew him too well, and her own smile faded as she crossed the room to join him.

'What's wrong?' Perching beside him she touched his chin, forcing him to meet her kind eyes. He couldn't resist them at sixteen and wasn't doing any better at thirty.

'My Aunt Maria.' He swallowed hard. 'Uncle Antonio suffered a serious heart attack yesterday and he's asking to see me.' Nico's voice trailed away and his awareness settled on her soft hand in his and the light, hypnotising scent rising from her warm skin.

'Of course. You'll go first thing in the morning?'

He nodded and stroked her cheek, sighing as she leaned into him.

'Book two seats. I'll come with you.' Her shy blush made his heart clench. 'If you want me to, that is?'

Nico pressed his mouth against her warm lips, sinking them into a long, luxurious kiss. 'Do you really need to ask? But what about your work?'

'I'll sort it out with Sadie. I'd already warned her we were going to make the trip, so it's only a question of bringing it forward. She'll be good.'

'You're such a terrible liar. It shows here,' he touched her flushed cheekbones, 'and here,' pointing to the corners of her eyes. 'Sadie will be mad I'm sure.'

She shrugged and he pulled her into his arms.

'I love you, Tish Carlisle.' Reluctantly he eased from their embrace. 'I need to get online and book our tickets. I'll leave you to sort out the famous Sadie.'

'I won't tell her now — she might be more mellow in the morning if your friend Jake performs well tonight.' Tish grinned.

'Did I miss something going on there?' He listened, bemused, as Tish updated him with their friends' plans.

'The sly old devil.' With one more kiss he reluctantly let her go. 'Get dressed before I forget what I'm supposed to be doing.' A wave of sorrow swept over him.

'We'll do this together,' she assured him and bent to give his cheek a gentle kiss before she walked away.

★ ★ ★

The second he spotted the snow-covered peak of Mount Etna out of the plane window, Nico's stomach churned and memories slammed into him. At thirteen he'd stared out of the window and fought back tears as the island faded into the distance. He couldn't have imagined it would be nearly twenty years before he'd return. He gave a start as Tish's warm hand squeezed his.

'Are you ok?'

Nico shrugged. 'I suppose so. I've imagined this so many times, but . . . ' He shook his head, unable to put into words the overwhelming sensations fighting for control of his emotions. 'My cousin, Guido, is meeting us. I know it's been an exhausting journey but do you mind if we go to the hospital first?'

'Of course not. I slept most of the way through the main flight to Milan, after all.' She grinned and he reached over to tweak her nose.

'You mean all the snoring I heard was you?'

'I do not snore,' she jested with fake annoyance. She snaked herself into his arms and Nico took advantage, pulling her to him for a much-needed kiss. He trailed his hand down over the fall of her glossy, black hair, lured by the faint lingering scent of the lemon shampoo she'd used before they left.

'Thanks again for coming — I'm pretty sure I couldn't do this alone,' he murmured softly as they came in to land.

The second he stepped off the plane Nico's senses went into overdrive. The warm flower-scented air, the barrage of Italians talking and gesticulating around them and the roar of nearby traffic brought him to a standstill. Tish's hand sneaked through his arm and her encouraging smile helped to get him moving again.

'Ciao, Nico!' Suddenly he was seized in a bear hug and kissed on both cheeks.

'Guido?' He stared at the massive, bearded man with laughing eyes and tried to reconcile him with the scrawny teenager he remembered. They'd grown up together, and he'd often ridden through the narrow streets of Catania on the back of his cousin's moped.

'Is your Papa — ' He couldn't force the words out.

'He's a little better today. Mamma's sure it's because you're coming.' He rested a large hand on Nico's shoulder.

Suddenly remembering Tish, Nico pulled her forward to introduce them. 'Guido, you'd better take it easy driving so you don't scare my lady too much.'

'Don't tell me the English have turned you into a wimp?' Guido's broad, white-toothed smile eased Nico's anxiety a touch. 'Come on. I'll have you there in fifteen minutes or be ashamed of myself.' He led them out through the terminal and over to his car, an Alfa Romeo identical to Nico's apart from the fact that it was a bright, in-your-face, glossy scarlet.

'Going up in the world, I see.' He gave a nod to Guido's car. 'Cara, Tish, do you mind sitting in the back? Your shorter legs won't suffer as much from being squashed.'

'Charming, I'm sure,' she responded with a sly grin. 'I'll get my own back on you later.'

'I've no doubt about that,' Nico quipped. They set off and he suppressed a smile at Tish's strangulated scream as Guido wove through traffic at high speed, cursing and waving his hands as he gave a running commentary on other drivers' ineptitude. As they screeched to a halt at the hospital she exhaled loudly.

'I'll park and come and join you. Just ask for the Intensive Cardiac Unit.' Guido's face was suddenly creased with worry.

* * *

'Nico?' Antonio's raspy voice croaked out the word and Tish saw Nico's jaw tighten. She could see the resemblance between them, although the older man's skin was an unhealthy grey.

'You didn't have to go to these lengths to get me to come back here, you know.' Nico attempted a light-hearted tone.

'It worked, though, didn't it?' his uncle declared and tried to pull himself up, only to be scolded by his wife, a voluptuous dark-haired woman fussing at the other side of the bed. 'Don't get

311

old, my boy,' he added wryly. 'Women think they can order you around.'

A faint smile pulled at Nico's taut mouth and he turned to Tish, gesturing for her to come closer.

'Zio, Uncle, I brought someone to meet you. This is Tish Carlisle. She's . . . special to me.'

Tish flushed under his uncle's hooded gaze as his dark eyes examined her. He nodded towards Nico.

'She's beautiful and a good woman, I can tell. Take her home. Elena's waiting for you.'

Nico's hand went rigid in hers and Tish caressed his fingers, trying to reassure him he wasn't alone. He muttered something in Italian and turned to her in apology.

'Sorry, sweetheart. I can't believe Elena's still around,' he whispered.

'Who is she?' Tish asked but he'd seemingly lost his ability to speak and Nico's aunt replied instead.

'She was housekeeper and nanny when Nico was a boy. After the accident the home was closed up. Now she has an apartment in Catania but goes regularly to take care of things. She heard Nico was arriving and she couldn't bear for him to return to an empty house.'

Tish yearned to wrap Nico in her arms and ease the pain evident in every taut line of his body.

'Shall we go, honey?'

He stared at her, unseeing for a few blank moments until he focused again and gave a brief nod.

'Do you mind, Uncle?'

'Go. Get some rest. Guido will take you.'

'I'd rather drive myself, if there's a car I can use?' Nico glanced around and Maria held out a set of keys.

'Take mine, it's the red Fiat parked by the far side wall.' She touched his hand. 'Be careful, Nico, my boy. It's been a long time.' It was obvious she referred to more than the roads.

'I will,' he promised, giving her a soft kiss on both cheeks.

Five minutes later Tish sat next to him, her hands folded neatly in her lap, waiting for him to find the emotional strength from somewhere to start the last leg of his long journey home.

'You'll be alright,' she murmured.

He turned to her, his dark eyes burning. 'Don't promise me that. My parents said the same and they were wrong.'

He fired up the car and pulled away with squealing tyres, glaring at the road. Tish clung to the door handle as he headed out of the city, his foot pressed to the floor. After a few minutes he slowed and relaxed his death grip on the steering wheel.

'Sorry.' He didn't look at her but she caught a slight upturn in the corner of his mouth. 'We'll be there soon.'

He made several more turns on the narrow, winding roads, then one onto a dead-end street before he stopped in front of a large, white house surrounded by high, bright red railings.

Nico leaned forward, staring. 'How

come it looks the same?'

The gates swung open and a short, stocky woman, her dark hair streaked with grey, walked towards them. Nico leapt out.

'Nico, my baby, you've come home at last.'

The woman held out her arms and he fell into them with a heart-wrenching sob.

Tish watched helplessly as Nico fell apart.

27

'This was my mother's favourite place to sit when she wasn't busy gardening.' Nico glanced around the sheltered patio and Tish knew he didn't see it as it was today, with its air of benign neglect, but as it was when his family was whole. 'The scent is always intoxicating in the evening, after the sun's warmed the flowers all day. She grew the red hibiscus over there from a cutting she took from my grandmother's garden.'

He gestured towards a lush, overgrown patch of tropical flowers beside the winding path leading down from the house.

'It's beautiful.' She held his hand, stroking gently, as they sat next to each other in white-painted wrought-iron chairs, looking out over the glistening Mediterranean Sea. She'd left him alone with Elena after they arrived and waited anxiously until he rejoined her, wrung out after a long conversation but more at peace than she'd ever seen him.

'It is.' Nico turned to her. 'I hadn't let myself remember.'

'And now?' she probed.

'I can enjoy it again. It still hurts, but in a comforting way, if that makes sense.' He leaned forward, pushing away the lock of thick hair which always fell across his forehead.

'I felt similar when I returned to Beach Road.' Tish tripped over her words and a rush of heat warmed her face. 'I'm not trying to compare the situation, but — '

He stopped her with a soft kiss.

'Don't apologise. You lost your beloved father twice over.' The dark, beautiful words slashed through her heart and tears rolled down her face. Nico brushed them away and pulled her over to sit in his lap, cradling her while she sobbed.

'I'm supposed to be comforting you,'

she gulped, giving unladylike sniffs.

'Oh, cara mia, my dear, you do that every day, just by breathing, by existing in my world again.' He rubbed gentle circles on her back and gradually her breathing steadied. 'Elena left us a light meal in the kitchen before she went home. After we've eaten, I'll ring the hospital to check on my uncle and if he's holding his own we'll wait until the morning to go back. He needs his rest, and so do we.'

'Yeah, you're right.'

'I always am — except when I'm wrong, of course.' A faint grin lit up his handsome face and a layer of Tish's weariness and worry fell away. 'Come on, let's go in.'

He eased her up to stand and they walked back inside, wrapped up in each other and their thoughts.

★   ★   ★

Quietly Nico opened the wooden blinds, hoping the morning sunlight

318

wouldn't wake Tish but needing to imprint the view back on his mind. He'd purposely chosen this room last night because it had been their old guest room, and so didn't harbour too many disturbing memories. In addition, it had the best view from the front of the house — straight up Mount Etna.

The crisp, blue sky framed the mountain, still topped with snow in the middle of summer. He leaned against the glass revelling in memories of one of the volcano's regular eruptions happening one Christmas Day when he was a child. He'd thought it a fireworks show put on specially for the holiday, the red sparks firing into the night sky and rivers of glowing lava snaking down the sides of the mountain.

The trouble with denying a large chunk of his life had been that he'd shut out the good as well as the painful. From now on, he intended to embrace both.

When Tish awoke, he'd take her for a walk down to the village and they'd have coffee and an almond pastry at his favourite café. It would still be there; the rhythm of life changed little on the island. The only difference was that Signor Carmatti would surely be retired by now and his son Placido, with whom Nico had been to school, would no doubt be running the business.

A niggling worry entered his head as Nico realised he still hadn't followed through on his promise to tell Tish everything. How would he cope if she turned on him and refused to understand? He'd dragged the packet of letters all the way from Cornwall to Las Vegas and now to Sicily, telling himself he was waiting for the right moment.

'Why are you frowning? It's a beautiful day, and I'm not tired any more.' Tish's light, teasing voice snaked into his awareness and Nico glanced around as she raised her arms to peel off her gauzy white nightdress.

'I'll tell you later. It can wait,' he grinned, 'but I can't.'

Nico shoved off the loose pyjama

320

trousers he'd slept in and joined her in the bed. He ran his hands over her warm, smooth skin, cupped her lush breasts and stroked lower until he made her gasp. 'Delizioso.'

'Please, Nico,' she moaned, her hips jerking as he blew gently on her heated skin. 'More.'

He slid up to cover her with his body, trapping her between his legs and rubbing sinuously against her. 'Is that what you want more of?'

She cursed him in a whisper, arousing him further with her desperation. Nico seized her mouth, drowning in her sweet taste. He'd never get enough of this woman as long as they both lived. He reached over her shoulder to grab a foil packet from the nightstand and leaned back to see to protecting her. He eased her legs apart and snuggled between them.

'Now, Nico, for God's sake, or I'll — ' He quieted her with a deep kiss and very slowly pressed into her, sliding into her welcoming body with a groan of excruciating pleasure. He pulsed in a steady rhythm, encouraging her with him all the way. He stared down into her vibrant eyes as they widened and flashed with desire. She was so close, and he needed to watch her fall apart. He withdrew nearly all the way, then slid his hand between them and pressed his fingers in the perfect spot as he slammed back into her, capturing her scream in his mouth as he collapsed in his own release.

Their bodies moulded together as one, trembling with the aftershocks of their passion and Nico caressed her face, dropping kisses all over her glistening skin. 'Sei cosi bella, you're so beautiful.' She reached up and mirrored his actions, ending at his mouth and taking him into her sweetness again.

* * *

Sitting on a wooden bench in the corner of the garden, Tish felt her stomach clench as Nico stalked across the grass towards her, his face dark as the midnight sky. He waved a handful of papers in her face and her heart sank, recognising the newspaper cuttings on the Penwarrens' deaths. She must not have put them away properly after re-reading them this morning while he was in the shower.

'Playing detective, are you? Why have you been checking up on my foster parents? Why didn't you just ask me?' he pleaded, sounding more hurt than angry.

'Nico, sit down.' She patted the bench, mentally counted to ten and struggled to stay calm as he perched on the edge of the seat. She'd lay her cards on the table, there was no choice. 'You've always been so prickly about your past — and something Annie and I discovered meant I had to know.'

'Annie? What's she got to do with anything?' He frowned, sounding puzzled.

'When we were going through my father's papers we read the diaries he left behind.' A wave of emotion swept over her but she forced it down. 'I've put off sharing this with you but you need to know. My father and Elaine Penwarren — ' Suddenly he seized her hand and fixed his molten eyes on her.

'Oh, amore mio, my love, I know already but I didn't want to tell you either.' He gave a rough laugh and shoved his hand through his hair.

'How long have you known?'

A tinge of colour highlighted the sharp planes of his long, narrow face. 'Since she died. William blamed your father for causing her death and made Peter and myself promise never to have anything to do with you or your family again. You'd left me heartbroken and I never expected to see you again, so it wasn't a hard promise to make. I tried to forget you by throwing myself into work and my painting, but nothing worked. Other women certainly didn't.' The irony in his voice touched her heart.

'When you returned and all my

feelings for you came flooding back, I rang Peter and he told me never to forget what your father did. I tried to tell myself it wasn't our fault, but inside I hated myself for being so weak around you. It tore me apart.'

His simple, heartfelt words sent a confusion of emotions rushing through Tish's head. Logically it shouldn't have mattered if he truly loved her, but Nico was a deeply honourable man and would have viewed his attraction to her as a betrayal of the people who had helped put his life back together.

He squeezed her hand. 'I've been a mess ever since you turned up in my office, twice as beautiful as I remembered and stirring me up with your flirtatious smile and soft voice.'

'So why the change of heart? For some reason you're OK with things now. I have a deep respect for your loyalty to your family and wouldn't have you any other way, but I'm still wondering.'

Nico let go of her hands and reached

into his jacket pocket to pull out a large white envelope.

'Peter came to see me a couple of weeks ago because he'd been given a pile of letters by his Aunt Marlene. William's brother, Jack, emigrated to the States back in the Seventies and they wrote every week. William told him everything.'

Tish paled. She'd read enough of her father's diaries to know she didn't want to hear any more details.

'You're welcome to read them yourself, but the gist of it is that Elaine was seriously ill and the drugs she was given caused a lot of emotional highs and lows as part of their side effects. They altered her behaviour and made her act out of character. The affair with your father was one.'

'He was a lonely man in an unhappy marriage,' she murmured sadly.

'I know, and I truly believe he made her happy for a while, although it destroyed his marriage when they were discovered. William stood by Elaine when she told him the truth, and never got over her death. He wanted revenge. After his first heart attack he knew he didn't have long, so extracted the promise from us boys. It was irrational to blame your father but he was past reasoning with, and Peter and I never knew the full story until now.'

She picked up his strong, competent hand and stroked his long, artist's fingers. 'They took away so much time from us.'

'I thought that for a while too — but we were young. We'd probably have been stupid and broken up and gone off with other people anyway. We've grown up, discovered passions which fire us up every day — and I hope you feel the same way, because I'm ready now.'

'For what?' Her heart raced as he dropped onto one knee.

'This.' Nico pulled a small, black, velvet box from his trouser pocket and flipped it open. Tish gaped at the large, square-cut diamond ring as he picked up her hand.

'Will you marry me? I know we need to sort out logistics but I can paint anywhere, and whatever makes you happy I'll do.' He beseeched her with his eyes. 'Put me out of my misery, please.'

'Oh, yes, yes, a thousand times yes! I dreamed of this when I was sixteen. It's been worth waiting for, but no longer. Put on that gorgeous ring immediately, then kiss me and we'll sort the rest out later.'

'Happy to obey, amore mio, you've always been my love and you're stuck with me now.' He slid the ring onto her finger, kissing it in place.

'It works both ways.'

'Good.' Nico wrapped her in his arms and did exactly as she instructed.

28

'Don't fuss, Nico, I'm not made of glass. Believe it or not, other women have had babies before me.' Playfully Tish pushed his hand away as he tried to help her up from the sun lounger.

'Not mine, they haven't.' He glowered, but it only lasted for a split second. Nowadays he couldn't be intimidating if he tried — marriage and impending fatherhood had turned him into the biggest softie ever.

'Good. I need to go and get these new designs sent off to Sadie or she'll be on the phone bugging me again.' She gathered up her sketchpad, reluctant to leave the sunny patio where she'd been working under the shade of a parasol all afternoon. They'd spent their first Christmas here in Sicily and never got around to leaving. 'I love this — passing on the hard side of things to her to sort out.'

'You don't miss it too much, do you?' Nico's concern tugged at her heart. He'd hounded her with questions for weeks before she sold her share of the business to Sadie, afraid she might regret it, but she'd made her choice and never looked back.

'Not at all. I have the freedom to concentrate on designing — and trust me, after the LA trade show I was so relieved to leave. I'll have to go to events occasionally to stay in touch with the direction things are going, but it won't be any more than I absolutely have to.'

'Good. I miss you when you're not around.'

Nico reached out to stroke her swollen belly through the thin raspberry silk dress. 'God, you're beautiful,' he told her. 'I've never seen anyone so lovely in all my life.'

His rasping voice aroused her beyond belief. At seven months and counting, she might see a whale reflected back in the mirror but with one sweep of her precious husband's gaze, she returned to being his passionate lover.

'A little different from my famous portrait.'

His skin flushed at her teasing words. Nico's last exhibition featured the painting of her and it had taken the art world by storm. She'd been so happy to see him enjoy the moment, giving up his anonymity with a light heart and even coming close to enjoying the notoriety.

'Don't you think it's time we travelled back to Trevayne if you want this to be a Cornish baby?'

She nodded and gave him a shy smile. 'Annie keeps asking when we're coming. I can't wait to see Jamie again — she says he's running around and talking now.'

'I'll get things organised and let Mrs Penlee know so she can get the house ready. Are you sure you don't want to buy somewhere larger? There's not much space.'

Tish shook her head. 'I love your cottage. It's special, and I can't imagine anything nicer than welcoming our baby there. It'll be interesting to see what happens when my mom comes and has to meet Annie. I think we'll have fireworks.'

He pulled her into his arms and dropped feather-light kisses all over her face.

'If they upset you, I'll turn back into mean Nico.' His words were softly spoken but she knew he meant them. Protective didn't begin to describe how he'd been since she showed him the positive pregnancy test a month after their honeymoon. Building a family of their own meant the world to him.

'I haven't seen him in a while.' She snaked her hands around his neck and wriggled up against him until he groaned. 'I appreciate you being considerate but I'm wondering whether you still fancy me?'

Tish pouted and a sudden flash of

desire lit up his eyes. She slid one hand between them and stroked him through his shorts, making him swell and harden at her touch.

'There's your answer, sweetheart,' he murmured. 'All you ever have to do is look at me and I'm all yours.'

He insinuated his fingers up under her skirt and teased her bare, warm skin, working his fingers in long, dangerous strokes until she writhed against him.

'I think it's nap time for pregnant ladies,' he breathed.

'A nap? That's not what I had in mind, you idiot.'

He chuckled, his warm laughter trickling through her veins.

'And you think I do? We might take a nap, but it'll be after I do wicked things to you.'

Tish beamed. 'Oh, good. I do love wicked, and you're an expert, Mr De Burgh.'

'You're pretty good yourself, Mrs De Burgh,' he growled and took her hand, pulling her towards the house. 'Siesta time.'

She didn't argue — though it was several long, wonderful hours before they gave in to sleep.

THE END

We do hope that you have enjoyed reading this large print book.

Did you know that all of our titles are available for purchase?

We publish a wide range of high quality large print books including:
Romances, Mysteries, Classics
General Fiction
Non Fiction and Westerns

Special interest titles available in large print are:
The Little Oxford Dictionary
Music Book, Song Book
Hymn Book, Service Book

Also available from us courtesy of Oxford University Press:
Young Readers' Dictionary
(large print edition)
Young Readers' Thesaurus
(large print edition)

For further information or a free brochure, please contact us at:
Ulverscroft Large Print Books Ltd.,
The Green, Bradgate Road, Anstey,
Leicester, LE7 7FU, England.
Tel: (00 44) 0116 236 4325
Fax: (00 44) 0116 234 0205

HUSHED WORDS

Angela Britnell

Cassie, a struggling single mother, and Jay, a wealthy financier, share a holiday romance in Italy; when fate throws them together again their sizzling passion rekindles. Cassie's family problems combined with Jay's fear of commitment and growing dissatisfaction with his lifestyle make their idea of a future together a dream. Jay can't ask for a second chance with Cassie until he discovers a new direction in life and lays it all on the line with the woman he loves.

TRUST IN ME

Rena George

When Kerra Morrison is named main beneficiary in her uncle's will, her cousins Sarah and David are furious their father favoured her over them. So when someone attempts to sabotage Kerra's new tearoom, her cousins seem to be the obvious culprits. But are there darker forces at work? The town's GP, Dr Duncan Crombie, comes to her aid. It would be easy to fall for such a man — if he didn't keep throwing up barriers every time they seem to be getting close . . .

DANGEROUS AFFAIR

Irena Nieslony

Feisty Eve Masters has had enough of the rat race. A successful career in London has allowed her to retire at forty-three and move to Crete. There, she falls for the handsome, but quiet, David Baker — but despite the mutual attraction, theirs is a volatile relationship. However, this is not the only thing to keep Eve occupied. The day she arrives, an English ex-pat estate agent is found murdered. Eve is intent on solving the crime — putting her own life in danger . . .